BUILDING CHARACTER

TALES FROM MONTANA

(and Other Damn Lies)

by

Dick Hoskins

W9-ACJ-833

Published by:

Polecat Press
612 West Haycraft
Coeur d' Alene, Idaho
83814

Library of Congress Catalog Card number 93-087436

ISBN 0-9639816-0-9

Acknowledgements

I am not sure that, when Dad set out to build my character, he expected to create such a weird character as I turned out to be. On the other hand, I don't know how he could have expected anything else, with such influences as H. B. Miller, Jess Wilson, Dad himself, and the other great story tellers in our neighborhood.

In addition to those liars--excuse me--story tellers, a great many other people influenced the contents of this book. To mention a few:

Marcia Rae Wells taught me grammar and sentence structure in the seventh grade, and I have never forgotten them, even though I break their rules right and left.

Writing instructors Larry Carlson and Linda Hutton offered positive criticism, advice and encouragement, in class and later on, also.

Jose' Tellez was the high level manager responsible for a company magazine. Jose' admired my yarns and insisted I keep writing them. He thought I should give them priority over that four-letter word, work.

Fellow writers in our Patrons of the Pen group and myriad other friends sampled my stories and asked for more.

Patrick MacManus inspired me, and gave me a number of helpful tips.

Extra special thanks go to Elizabeth Crummer for helping me select, edit and proofread the contents.

Most of all, though, I thank my wife, Dorothy, (The O'Reilly) who suffered through thousands of recitations of these and other stories, and still had the grace and patience to read and comment on the printed version. Why she puts up with me is beyond understanding.

A Non-Apology

This book is dedicated to my father, Ernest Moses Hoskins, who believed one should never let the truth stand in the way of a good story.

Ernie Hoskins respected the truth so much that he sometimes applied several coats of varnish to an unvarnished truth to ensure it was well preserved. If he encountered the naked truth, he always dressed it up to make it presentable. Any time he found a truth to be wrinkled or convoluted, he carefully stretched it into a proper shape.

Many of the stories herein are true. Should you doubt that, well, just peer through the varnish, and I'm sure you'll find, well-preserved, the grain of truth you're looking for. Of course, some of these pieces are lies and some of them are damn lies. Make up your own mind which is which.

Contents

Stinker

"There's a skunk in this tent!"

The Park Ranger's report that my announcement woke every camper within five miles is not at all true. Why, it hardly disturbed my dear wife at all. The O'Reilly just rolled over and said, "Go back to sleep. You were dreaming again."

I was not dreaming. When I felt pressure on my legs and heard crackling from the bag of corn chips stored in the corner of the tent, I wondered why The O'Reilly was creeping around in the dark without her flashlight and why she was after corn chips at that time of night anyway. Then my olfactory nerves woke up and I quietly commented on their discovery. The skunk hurried out the door and I suppose the little critter exaggerated, too, when he told his mamma, "All of a sudden this monster started screeching. I got out of there with as much dignity as I could. I don't know why

1

he was so upset. All I wanted was one little corn chip. Geez, what a grouch."

This was not my first encounter with a Pepe' le Pew at that campground. Another time only a few years before we had had another visit from one of the varmints. It really was not the big deal The O'Reilly makes it out to be. She has told her version of the incident to some of our friends, but, bless her, she has not yet learned to tell a good yarn properly. If you're going to tell an out-and-out lie, you need to keep a perfectly straight face and remain nonchalant. Uncontrolled giggling and hysterical finger-pointing really detract from the tall tale you're telling.

On that occasion, the skunk came by at about ten-thirty at night. The O'Reilly had just gone into the tent to lay out her sleeping bag. She claims she heard a long piercing scream, and came out of the tent to find me dancing on the table like a Scotsman in front of a pay toilet, holding the camp lantern in one hand, shaking my finger at the skunk with the other, and chittering like a monkey. The *truth* of the matter is, I got up on the table to get a better picture of the critter. I just forgot that my camera was still in the car.

Now, I am *not* afraid of skunks. I do, however, suffer from a childhood trauma that left me with an extreme allergy to their odor. Even at long range, skunk odor causes me to break out in a sweat. My eyes bug out. I tremble a lot, particularly in my voice, since my vocal chords seem to tighten up. The O'Reilly says I become hysterical--her exact words are, "He goes off his nut,"-- but I'm only trying to get away from the odor.

My personal aversion began back about 1937 or so-- back when a prime skunk hide was worth from fifty cents to a dollar. That kind of money may not seem like much now, but when one considers that a man's wages were then a dollar a day and found, it brings the price into perspective. Especially since "found" meant that you could sleep any place in the barn you found warm, and if you found out what time meals were, you could share the family's grub. If there was any.

2

Dad told my friend Murdie and me all about skunks. Contrary to popular belief, skunks don't think of their weapon as perfume, nor do they use it reflexively. For instance, most skunks killed along the road die before they have a chance to do their worst. A skunk's arsenal is limited; he has just so much stink to use up, and when it's gone, he is, so to speak, a dead duck. He must live his life like a gunslinger with only six bullets left, so he uses his resources sparingly. When a skunk sprays you, he does it deliberately and with malice aforethought, and you should consider it a compliment that he thought you important enough to use up a bullet. (The skunks we encountered camping had no cause to waste a shot on us, and consequently, like most skunks, hardly smelled at all. That's why the little bastards could get into camp and even into our tent unnoticed.)

Murdie and I were beginning to realize, about that time, that our parents were at an awkward age. They were no longer the all-wise parents we had always known throughout our childhood, but they had not yet regressed to the idiocy of teenagers' parents. So, we believed the part Dad told us about a skunk's limitations, but either we didn't believe or conveniently forgot the part about the danger of fooling with them. As usual, that's where the trouble started.

During the winter (Dad told us) skunks don't really hibernate. They den up in the cold, but come out when it thaws. For a den, they dig a tunnel and snuggle up together with one's nose over another's flank, sort of stacked like shingles. Then they plug up the hole outside, and sleep through the bad weather. Since the dens are not very deep, it is easy to dig down to the line of skunks, shoot the first one (Dad said!), pick him up by the tail, shoot the next one, and so on. Since there might be a dozen or so skunks in the den, to dig through the frozen ground to get at them was worth the work.

Dad's lectures really got Murdie and me excited. I had already located a skunk den on the bank of the big irrigation canal that ran through our farm. It apparently was once a ground squirrel's diggings, but I

3

guess the skunks had enlarged it. During a thaw, I saw lots of skunk tracks in the slushy snow around it, but now that the weather was cold again, the entrance was plugged with grass. Just like Dad said.

Since the den was on the soft ditch bank, Murdie and I thought digging the skunks out would be easy. It wasn't. We had to dig through about four inches of frozen ground and three feet of unfrozen earth. We slaved half a day in near-zero cold to dig down to the first skunk. For a couple of eleven-year-olds, that was a lot of work and it took a lot of patience, but, eventually, there it was--a tail. And the attached skunk seemed undisturbed by the digging. We discussed, then, who should do the shooting (we'd both had .22 caliber rifles since before we were ten) and who should do the grabbing. I was no fool. We had *my* .22, so obviously Murdie was the one who had to take the bull, so to speak, by the tail.

The first skunk went right according to plan. We dug around it, I plinked it right behind the ear, and Murdie threw it out--about 30 feet. No smell. The second was harder, but not too bad. By that time, success had gone to our heads, and we were envisioning riches. The world was rosy.

I must have gotten careless with the next shot. I was leaning over the trench off-balance, and I didn't make a clean kill. This skunk, with malice afore-thought, curled up in pain, but at the same time let go. In the process of curling, he aimed the scent through an arc that included my face. I saw it coming and had time to close my eyes and yell. I should have kept my mouth shut.

When a person is cursing, spitting, vomiting, and crying all at one time, you'd think his best friend could refrain from laughing. Pretty soon, Murdie began to worry that I'd never breathe again and sobered up enough to begin to give me advice, though he couldn't bring himself to come near me. From a distance I finally heard him yelling at me.

"Roll down in the ditch", he said, "and wash some of it off."

4

Anything was better than the agony I felt, so I did as he suggested. My weight was just enough to break through the film of ice, and the frigid water actually felt good. It gave my brain something else to think about, anyway. Like, the arms and body are saying, "Hey, this kid is freezing to death!" and the nose is saying, "Who cares?"

You'd think a loving mother would let a wet, freezing, bawling kid come into the house by the fire. UH-uhhh! I spent the rest of the day confined to the bunkhouse, scrubbing. Every once in a while, Mother opened the door a crack, shoved in a different kind of soap, and said, "Here, try this," and slammed the door again. Dad said that tomato juice was supposed to take out the smell, so I bathed in home-canned tomatoes. The best I can say is that I smelled like polecat cacciatore. Somebody brought my bedding out and dumped it in front of the door, and I slept alone in the bunkhouse. Even my dog refused to stay out there with me.

The worst part was going to school. Farm kids never smelled very good. Cow and pig manure and old milk and slop were some of the minor odors in the schoolroom. But whenever I'd get warm, the air in our room was enough to make a grown man cry--and our teacher often did. The kids, naturally, called me "Stinker" the whole term, and after a while it got so it wasn't even worth fighting about. The only permanent effect was this allergy.

I am not *afraid* of skunks. I'm not afraid of a charging buffalo, or a coiled rattlesnake, or a dangling power line, either.

My Father's Day

My father and my Grandpa kept a cattle feeding lot
'Til prices fell in '28 and cost them all they'd got.
Bankruptcy killed my Grandpa, but my Daddy weathered
    through,
Decided that Montana had some farming he could do.

We lived a life of poverty, but so did all our friends.
But Dad was paying creditors; paid all and made
    amends.
He didn't tell me 'bout his past, just taught me honesty:
The only way to live if you would keep your conscience
    free.

As I grew up he'd say to me, "Let's stop and smell the
    flowers."
But then he'd work like driven slave, sometimes for
    sixteen hours.
"Don't ever let the truth stand in the way of a good yarn."
Advice like that he gave me while we worked around the
    barn.

"The work will wait, the fishing won't," is what he used
    to say.
We'd picnic in the mountains and enjoy a freedom day.
"Don't point a gun at anything you don't intend to shoot."
To fail to heed this rule, I knew, meant boost from leather
    boot.

They say as you grow older that your parent you become.
Prognostications such as that are frightening to some.
But I tell you it doesn't seem to me to be so bad.
When I grow old I'd like to be as wise as was my Dad.

Fit for a King

Ernie Hoskins (my Dad) lost *his* money when the stock market crashed in '28. This was long before it started raining investors on Wall Street. Dad was in *live* stock, and cattle prices dived early.

A year or so after the crash, Dad heard that the Northern Pacific Railway Company was offering free passage for farmers and their goods to some of the territory served by its lines. Ernie together with a tried and true friend, Grover Cochran, looked Montana over, and decided to move to the Flathead Indian Reservation in the Flathead Valley. So we moved to Montana and settled on 40 acres of rented hardpan clay, and lived in a *Log House*

We were poor. We were so poor we didn't feed the birds--they fed us. I think we survived. This is about the Log House.

It couldn't have been much of a house. I'll bet it was no more than 20 by 24 feet, including the lean-to shed that housed the kitchen. There were no rooms when we moved in--that is, there was *a* room when we moved in. The walls were made of logs six or eight inches through, flattened a little on each side with an adze, which did a pretty rough job. The cracks between the logs had (once upon a time) been chinked with mortar, but the mortar had long since loosened as the logs dried, and had fallen away in large chunks. Dad said that, before he fixed the place up, you could stand in the middle of the house and throw a cat through the cracks in any direction. That is one of the few times Dad exaggerated; it was only true of the North wall. Any cat worth his salt would have been able to hook a claw on one side or the other of a crack as he went through any of the other walls.

Some cheap boards around the inside of the logs cut the draft a little, and a partition across the middle, to form two "rooms", made the place home.

I don't remember what the floor of the main house was like. I guess there was one. I do remember the kitchen floor, though. It was dirt. Not dirty--*dirt*. It was great for playing marbles, but Mother objected to the kind of marble games that required holes. I played mostly bullseye.

The kitchen roof had originally been sodded over to improve the insulation, but a lot of the sod had eroded away, leaving only patches of dirt. Mustard and other weeds grew there in the spring, but by late summer the "sod" had dried up and the dust sifted through into the soup. Actually, it improved the flavor and probably the nutritional value of some of those soups we ate between 1930 and 1934.

The house sat back from the road, about 50 yards or so, in a pasture. There was no other front yard--the pasture was *it*. There were half a dozen crab apple trees in that front yard, and each year we'd gather washtubs full of crab apples and Mother made apple butter and applesauce. Some of those apples were the size of walnuts, but most were little ones. The apple butter was all right--Mother strained that--but she made applesauce with core, stem, skin, fur, feathers, and all. It had *body*.

A major irrigation ditch ran under the road and through the pasture (front yard) just west of the house. In the heat of summer, the water was probably eight or nine inches deep, and my sister and I played in it for hours. Our bathing suits were our old coveralls with the legs and sleeves worn clear off. We didn't learn to swim, but we could mud crawl pretty well

Huge cottonwood trees towered into the sky along the ditch. I used to climb way up in them and it seemed like I'd be 200 feet high. I could see everywhere. Only recently I was back in the Flathead and visited the old house. Funny, those trees are now only about 35 or 40 feet high. They must have shrunk in their old age. I guess we all do.

We lived at the Log House until 1934. While we lived there, we got our first dog, Pat. He got run over and Dad would have mercifully killed him, but we kids wouldn't let him, so Pat lived to a ripe old age. Pat got into a losing argument with a porcupine there, and we ate porcupine stew (Pat's revenge). We also ate muskrat and blackbird breasts. At the log house, I remember, I died the first time . Honest!!

But those are other stories

The Fine Art of Dreading

Of all the skills my father taught me, the most useful has to be the art of dreading. And properly dreading a distasteful chore is indeed an art. Being artistically inclined, I took up dreading readily and enthusiastically.

When it came time to do something he particularly disliked, Dad often said, "Wait. I gotta dread that a while first." On the farm there were a lot of distasteful chores to dread, and some of them even had to be dreaded several times a day. Like milking cows when the temperature was down around zero. No one should do a chore like that without the proper amount of dreading. If a person hadn't dreaded long enough, he might find he'd finished the job without being prepared to enjoy the associated misery properly. He might not be able to appreciate that gloriously refreshing feeling of snow falling down the back of his neck, the pungent perfume of fresh cow manure, the pain in stiff and almost frozen hands as he wrestled with the barn door. No, such things need to be dreaded, and dreaded wisely and thoroughly. We spent so much time dreading milking that it was a good thing we had only two cows. We wouldn't have had time to milk more.

Another task we particularly dreaded was changing the setting of the irrigation water when the mosquitoes were really bad. And they were really bad all summer long in Montana. First we had to dread putting on those old rubber boots. Boots somehow always hurt our feet. After we dreaded putting boots on, we dreaded slogging out through the fields with the mud trying to pull our boots off at every step. Then we dreaded having to drag a muddy piece of canvas from one place to another to dam a ditch. After that, we dreaded the work of shovelling the mud to hold the dam and divert the water evenly. Finally, we got around to dreading the mosquitoes. We dreaded the way they got in our eyes, and we dreaded the way they got up our noses, and, most of all, we dreaded the way they got in our mouths when we cussed them. Such advanced dreading makes one an expert.

Today I claim to be one of the Master Dreaders of my time. In fact, I'm so good at it that I sometimes dread chores until they no longer have to be done. This year I'm fixing to dread raking the leaves. If I do a good dreading job, maybe it will snow before I get to them, and I won't have to rake them till spring when I can dread the job all over again.

The Mistake

The blizzard had ended at nightfall, and with clearing had come the cold. Now the mercury huddled forlornly in the thermometer bulb, barely reaching the minus 40 mark. Even the morning sun, sighting between mountain peaks and etching an eye-tormenting fantasy of white on white, could not assuage the cold. In the town at the end of the valley, life seemed stilled, smoke rising from a single chimney on the main street. Across the front window of that building, curtained by fairy scrolls of frost, was stencilled the single word "Sheriff". Out front, the snow had drifted around a shiny black Model A Ford, the county's one official vehicle.

Inside, the Sheriff stoked the ancient woodstove and poured a cup of villainously black coffee from a simmering pot. He eased himself into the creaky office chair, swung his booted feet onto the desk and contemplated the cup, fondling its warmth with alternate hands, then flexing his fingers. Presently he drank and set the cup down carelessly. Twisting in the chair, he retrieved a huge clasp knife from his pocket and began studiously cleaning his fingernails.

He seemed not to hear the car that came squeaking through the new snow, until it stopped at the rear of the office. Then he raised his head and, knife poised, he watched the back door. Car doors slammed and feet crunched through the snow, then the door opened to admit two men and a woman. The Sheriff rose courteously to his feet, but sat back down immediately. One of the men was short, round and well-dressed, and the Sheriff unconsciously pinned the label "Dude" on him. The other man was pale and slightly stooped. He gave the Sheriff a familiar wave.

"Good morning, Yo," he said.

"Hello, John," the Sheriff said, "What can I do for you? Got some trouble?"

"You bet he has!" crowed the little Dude. "He sold alcohol to an Indian!"

12

The Sheriff turned slowly and looked the little man up and down. His mouth pursed as if it wished to be rid of a bad taste.

"Who're you?" the Sheriff asked.

"Claude Empers, U. S. Treasury Agent." The little man produced a badge. "I caught this man selling alcohol to this woman. Lock him up and I'll send a Marshall for him."

"John selling alcohol--aw, I can't believe that."

"Here's the evidence," the little man said, dragging a small bottle from his coat pocket.

The Sheriff took the bottle and traced the words on the label with the point of his knife. His lips moved as he read. The little round man leaned forward eagerly, as if wanting to help with the reading. Finally, the Sheriff raised his head and spoke.

"Cough medicine?"

"Twenty percent alcohol," said the little man. "Worse than wine!"

"Oh sh--shucks!" the Sheriff said, with a glance at the woman. Then to her, "You Indian?"

"One fourth." She spoke softly, but stood proudly.

"Belong to the tribe?"

"Yes."

"This man give you money to do this?"

The woman shook her head, but her proud stance melted.

"Um-hum," the Sheriff said.

"Well, lock him up," the fat little man insisted.

The Sheriff rose slowly to his feet. He was not really a tall man, but he seemed to tower over the little fat man.

"You may be who you say you are--a Federal Agent. But you're worse than that. You are a God Damn Fool." The agent tried to speak, but the Sheriff leaned over him. "I've known John Johnson for nine--ten years?--and there isn't a more honest or law-abiding man in this country. You maybe tricked him into selling alcohol to an Indian. Maybe he broke the law. That's not the point. I know John, and other folks know John, and when word of this gets out, you won't be safe in the state of Montana

"Don't you threaten a United States Agent," the little man said, puffing himself out.

The Sheriff snorted a suppressed laugh.

"John," he said, "who else knows you're here?"

"Lee Collins. I asked him to tell Nellie."

"Asked him? Why didn't you?"

"Mr. Empers wouldn't let me. We just got in the car and came here."

"Oh Great Jesus!" the Sheriff said. He looked at the clock. "It'll take 'em fifteen, twenty minutes to get together, but they'll make better time. They know the road, and they'll be madder than hell." He turned to the little man. "You listen to me! You get your ass and your Indian into your car and get out of here. Take the East road around the Lake. I'll try to stop them here, but if I can't I'll tell 'em you took the West road. Git!"

"What're you saying?"

"I told you I've known John for near ten years. I know that town, too--used to farm there myself. Half the folks there would have starved out these hard years, but John gave 'em credit and always believed in 'em. Hell, he helped me more times than I can count. People in that town God Damn near worship him, and they all know he's honest as the day is long. When they hear he's been picked up on a trumped up charge, the whole town'll be here to see about it. And when they hear you didn't even give John time to tell his wife--well, Collins is bad enough, but he'll go to Miller and Jordan and they're *real* hot-heads. You made two mistakes, and if you don't get out of here, they'll *hang* you."

"You wouldn't let them do that! " the little Agent said.

The Sheriff thought for a moment before he answered. Then he smiled with his teeth. "I guess I wouldn't try to stop guys who can shoot like Collins and Miller. If they took you, I'd have to call for help, and I'd have to charge them with murder." He stopped and stared vacantly at the frosty window. Presently he leaned

14

over the little man again. "You filthy pipsqueak," he said through his teeth. "I'd rather be with them. But I'm Sheriff, so I got to get you out alive. Now get in your car and *get*. Or by God, I may throw this badge away."

"Wait until Washington hears about this," the little man screamed. "Come on, Johnson. Come on, Carrie."

The Sheriff put his hand on Johnson's arm and shook his head. The sound of cars growling through the snow came from the street in front. The Sheriff walked to the front window and scratched a hole in the frost to peek out. "Oh God!" he said Then he spoke sharply. "John", he said, "get busy with a cup of coffee. You," to the little man, "out the back door. Now! That's Collins and Jordan. Collins has a deer rifle. Somebody's got a rope. Move. Move fast!"

The little man hesitated. The Sheriff picked him up by collar and pants seat and tip-toed him to the back door, then took the woman by the arm and pushed her out, closing the door after her. He went back to the stove, poured hot coffee over the remains in his cup, sat down with his feet up, and resumed his manicure, lifting his head only to listen as a car started,then drove away, the sounds of its engine fading slowly.

The front door crashed open and half a dozen men crowded in.

"Mornin', gents," the Sheriff said placidly. "Come in and shut the door."

The men seemed uncertain in their anger. One, carrying a rifle at ready, stepped forward and spoke.

"We came about Johnson. We--"

"John's right there." The Sheriff pointed with his knife.

"Where's that son of a bitch that brought him here?" Growled assents came from the crowd at the door.

"Him? Oh, he left a while back. Seems he made a mistake. Say, you guys mind giving John a ride back home?"

"We want that dude!" shouted the spokesman.

"Now, Pete," the Sheriff stood up and fed wood to the stove. "You fellas got better things to do than chase around on these roads in the cold. By the way--roads all clear down your way?"

"Dammit, Joe," said the man addressed as Pete, "you know what we came for."

"Yeah, Pete, I do. Can't say as I blame you. Mighta done the same thing in your place. But he's gone, so you might as well go home. First, though, it's gonna be a cold ride, so why don't you all come in and get warm while I make some more coffee. Oughta be enough cups around here somewhere."

Still grumbling, the men drifted forward and re-formed around the stove. Soon the angry muttering melted into good-natured cursing of the cold . They drank coffee cheerfully, and before long they filed out, Johnson a hero among them. The Sheriff watched the cars out of sight, then turned back to his desk and took up a framed picture of a pretty but not-so-young woman.

"Betty," he said to her, "you wouldn't believe what it takes to do the sheriffing around here." He laid the picture down faceup, and began to laugh. He laughed and laughed until he sat sobbing, his head on his arms, his tears falling on the picture before him.

On Eating Porcupine

I've heard (and it may even be true) that the porcupine is a protected species in the Canadian Northwest. The theory is that Ole Porky is an emergency food supply that an unarmed man, running short (or out) of food in the cold North, could kill with a club. Supposedly, he could eat the porcupine and survive.

I doubt it.

As usual, the bureaucrats know not whereof they speak. In the first place, Ole Porky is usually found in *his* first place--a tree. Now, how is an unarmed person, presumably weak from hunger--going to get him down? As for killing him with a club--well, maybe. If there's no snow. In deep snow, a porcupine can usually tunnel faster than a *strong* man can wallow along, let alone a man weakened with hunger. And if he *did* get a crack at the porcupine, the snow would cushion the blow so it won't do much good (or harm, from Ole Porky's point of view).

Even if our starving hero does manage to kill the beast, he still has to *eat* it to survive, and I submit that *that* is a fate worse than death.

17

About 1932 or 3, a porcupine wandered down from the Mission Mountains and found his way to our farm. That's what we called the forty acres of Montana hardpan Dad was trying to scrape a living from. My old dog Pat was, at the time, very young, ambitious, and not overly smart. But he saw his duty and he dood it--he staunchly defended us from the ravening beast. Ole Porky slapped him up alongside the head with his tail. Good old persistent Pat turned the other cheek--and got that one full of quills, too. By the time Dad got there to help, Pat had more quills than the porcupine.

Dad pulled out quills until he was tired, then left the rest to grow out. Some of them took 15 years. Dad decided that the porcupine represented *meat*. We didn't have a lot of that in those days, so Dad skinned the varmint out and brought the carcass home for Mother to cook. That's when the trouble started.

I don't remember how cold that day was, but I do remember that I got pretty chilled standing around outside. Why didn't I go inside? Because that's where Mother was cooking the porcupine, that's why! That porcupine *stank*! The sour smell crept into your mouth when you breathed, and seeped into your eyes when you held your breath. It was awesome! I don't remember what the season was, but if it wasn't fall, that smell was the reason the leaves fell off the trees. But--we ate porcupine stew. There are worse things, but please don't pin me down as to what they might be.

I suggest that, if you are ever out in the woods and cold and starving and you have occasion to hunt porcupine with a club, *don't*. Eat anything else. Eat the tree the porcupine's in. Eat the club. Or just sit down under the tree and waste away. That would be one heck of a lot more pleasant than cooking a @#%*# porcupine, let alone eating it.

The Shooter

Nobody supposed that a woman who was a scant five feet tall and might have weighed a hundred pounds soaking wet and had never even held a gun could shoot so effectively. But women in those days often came up with the unexpected.

Mother's hundred pounds assayed out at about equal parts of grit, bias, pride, loyalty, stubbornness, temper, volatile sense of humor, and self-pity. She was a city girl who had taught school and clerked in a county courthouse. When she married Dad, she knew little about farming and its vagaries, less about cooking and nothing about guns. Eventually, she learned quite a bit about farming.

After Dad went bankrupt in 1928, his sister-in-law thought she should control Dad and Mother's financial and personal lives. There are some fairly obscene similes to describe how that went over with my proud and stubborn mother. When Dad suggested we move to an Indian Reservation in Montana to live on forty acres of hardpan that was laughingly called a farm, I suspect Mother jumped at the chance to be dirt-poor but free of Dad's relatives. Poor Grandma Riley bade her daughter a tearful goodbye. "I'll never see you again," she said. "Those Indians will scalp you." Turns out, the Indians should have been warned about Mother.

Dad raised enough on that hardpan farm to feed two cows and a team of horses but not a family, so most of the time, he labored for the United States Reclamation Service. Our neighbors were wonderful people, excepting the closest ones. The neighbor to the west was such a master of invective that Dad, no slouch himself, looked on him (listened to him) with awe. One didn't have to listen very loud. That man's voice carried over that quarter mile winter, summer, spring and fall. The neighbor to the south had several dogs that ran loose, as all farm dogs did. These, however, took to chasing horses and cattle for fun. Dad held the opinion that a stock-chasing dog was worthless, and might as well be shot, and that the owner who kept such a varmint was trash that came pretty close to being eligible for the same sentence.

One day the dogs were running our horses and Mother was in a less than happy mood. What woman wouldn't be with too little food, a dirt floor in her kitchen, two snivelling brats (my sister and me) and her nearest neighbors not the kind she wanted truck with? Mother put up with the dogs running the cow, but she was inordinately proud of that team of horses.

We kids were aware that Mother knew little about guns and was afraid of them, so when she began to swear and took down the double barrelled shotgun, we hid out. For all we knew, she might be after us. She wasn't, though. She marched down to the creek, hiked up her dress, kicked off her shoes and waded through the muck to the fence around field where the dogs were running. My sister and I tagged along some distance behind, wondering what was going to happen. Mother rested the gun on a fence post and fired at the dogs.

Since she had never asked, Dad had never told her that she should never cock both barrels at once. The mechanism was worn so that firing one barrel made the other hammer fall too. Mother fell backward from the double recoil and sat down, hard. J. R. Williams once drew an "Out Our Way" cartoon showing a pioneer woman who'd run a bear off with a double barrelled shotgun. The woman is wondering if she ran up a doctor bill saving the pigs. That cartoon is one of my favorites; I always think of Mother.

Mother's double killed two dogs outright, and a third died later. My sister and I stood trembling when Mother got up and turned toward us. She was shooting dogs, and we were sure our dog Pat would be next. We threw our arms around Pat and begged Mother not to shoot him. She looked at us, started to laugh, then came over to us, rubbing her shoulder, the shotgun under her arm. She hugged us, petted the dog and told us not to worry about him. She was cheerful and singing all that afternoon.

After Dad came home that evening, tired and dirty from operating the business end of a shovel all day, the neighbor showed up to complain about the loss of his dogs. He might have been better off confronting Mother and the shotgun. Dad was strong on loyalty too, but his long suit was his temper. I think that, if that neighbor to the west had been listening, he might have learned a few new words. I did.

Our southern neighbor never spoke to us again, but his dogs never ran our stock again, either.

Requiscat

I went to a funeral yesterday.
I didn't mean to. It was just there when I arrived.

The mourners, glistening black in the morning sun,
Came and left in groups.
Some bustled about,exhorting the corpse to return to life.
Some stalked in silent dignity beside the bier.

The others came, and screamed their rage at me,
Not for what I had done, but because I was not one of
        them
They cursed at me until I ran away.
Then they followed, taunting, and I hear their jeers still
        ringing round me.

I don't know whose the lifeless body was.
He may have been a brother, son, a leader.
I don't know what claimed his life--
Old age, a denizen of the night,
One of my kind or one of his own.
I didn't care enough, so I didn't stop to ask.

I doubt that those who jeered at me either knew or
        cared.
But, yet, perhaps they were right.
He was of their kind and I of mine,
And because I didn't care enough,
I am their enemy.

Soon, the crows flew away about their business,
And I was left to walk alone and wonder.

Old Thunder

Most dogs are afraid of thunder, I guess. There must be some deep, distant racial memory of a catastrophe that causes the first little rumble to send a dog scurrying for cover in slavering, wide-eyed terror. On the other hand, maybe thunder just hurts their ears.

My old dog, Pat, had a racial memory and his own memories, and when he'd crowd under my bed before and during a mild thunder storm, his terrified shivering shook the bed at about 4.0 on the Richter scale, with peaks, at the louder crashes, at 5.4. Sometimes, staying in bed was difficult, and sleeping was downright impossible.

I've already told you about the log house. Besides the cracks between the logs, there were the ill-fitting sash windows. Some of them were so tight that they couldn't have been opened with dynamite. That was all right--the cracks around them were big enough so air and mosquitoes could circulate freely. But there was no middle ground. Any window that could be opened rattled around loosely, and the sash had to be propped up with the proper length of stick. The windows must have been installed by a near-sighted midget, so the sills were about a foot and a half from the ground, and the upper panes were so low that anyone over five feet tall (my mother wasn't) had to stoop to look out.

Pat was a nearly grown pup in the summer of '31. He slept outside. Heck, there wasn't enough room for even us human people inside. That's until the night Pat was nearly fatally attacked by a thunderstorm.

We slept through the early part of the storm. Pat had probably whined and scratched at the door when the storm first came over the hill to the west, but we hadn't heard him. As the storm loomed up over him, Pat became desperate, and he circled the house looking for a safe haven.

Now, ordinarily, Pat was a well-behaved dog, and he would never have even considered jumping though an open window. As things happened, he probably never considered it again. But this night, with desperation's claws clamped around his conscience, he had a choice of braving the storm or taking the coward's way through the window. I never said he was brave. He chose the window. The first we knew about it, we woke to his screams of mortal terror.

We tried to guess the sequence of events. Probably there was a rumble of thunder that presaged a loud crash. Pat fled through the window. His head knocked loose the stick that propped up the sash, and the sash fell before he got clear. He stopped short, his hind legs trapped.

Came the loud boom of thunder. Certain that Old Thunder had at last caught him, Pat beseeched all the gods he knew to save him from this private hell. His principal god (Dad) levitated from his bed with the pronouncement of "Bleepity bleep of a bleep" which was lost in poor old Pat's frantic howls. Lesser gods (my sister and I) rose from their beds and added their wails of distress in sympathy with Pat.

Pat was never the same. True, his hair didn't turn white. Oh, a shade or two lighter, maybe. And the humiliation and mental anguish of hearing hysterical laughter every time his near-fatal experience was mentioned must have been part of the reason for his inferiority complex.

As long as he lived (seventeen years), nothing ever convinced him that Old Thunder wasn't out to get him. Even his favorite activity--pheasant hunting--ended when thunder rumbled in the distance. Even a god can't shoot straight with a 5.4 earthquake pressing against his legs.

The Swamp

The boy sat with his back against the big willow, pondering life as he saw it. In the heat of the July afternoon, everything had nearly come to a stop. The cows and horses all stood as still as possible, their tails languidly brushing at the ever-present flies, enduring the heat, waiting for the cool of sundown. His cat sprawled in the damp grass under the huge rose bush. Even the chickens lay gasping in their dust wallows in the shade of the outbuildings. Only the dog was alert, lying relaxed and panting, but watching his Lord and Master's every move.

The boy was bored. His father worked in the fields, as usual, despite the heat. His mother sought relief in sleep, and his sister was reading. She was *always* reading. For a girl of twelve that might be entertaining enough, but, heat or no heat, a nine-year-old boy needed action.

He stood up and strolled past the house to the row of trees beside the lane, and stood looking through the fence at the forbidden field to the north. The neighbor had put it in summer fallow. He'd plowed and harrowed it in the spring to kill most of the weeds, then left it dry and dusty and idle for the summer. The boy loved the whirlwinds that were spawned on the bare, hot field, and, whenever he could, he'd run into their swirling dust. Some of them were small and fiercely spinning, and they threw dirt and small stones and straw at him hard enough to sting. Others towered to the sky, large and stately, seeming to spin slowly. The boy would run to the center, and, moving with the quiet eye, he'd watch miniature twisters form and die in each rotation of the huge outside ring.

At the east side of the field lay The Swamp, a great marsh of cattails which he considered unexplored. He was forbidden to go into it, and thus it was ever beckoning. No satisfactory reason for the restriction had ever been given him. "Because I say so" only made him more curious, and he and the friends who occasionally came to visit and play imagined various terrors that must be too awful for the grownups to tell. Perhaps there was quicksand, or maybe wild animals. The most gratifyingly frightening explanation was originated by his best friend. There must be a crazy man living in the swamp, someone so depraved that to even see him was dangerous. Between them they created a most satisfactorily ruthless maniac, and embellished the idea until they both fully believed in him and lived in terror of him.

At the other end of the field was a pasture. The owner had loosed twenty or so beef cattle to feed on the pasture grass and to drink from the water of the swamp. The cattle--travelling single file like cattle everywhere-- had criss-crossed the fallow land with their trails. Those trails fascinated the boy. He imagined roads to adventures no one else knew or would ever know. But when a bull had been added to the cattle herd, the boy's city-bred mother had declared the whole field off limits to him, so he began to plan his incursions at the times when his parents were busy elsewhere. He had, however, absorbed enough of his mother's alarm that he always made sure the dog was along to defend him from the bull.

As he looked across the dry field, shimmering in the heat, a story grew in his mind--a tale of pioneers like his great-grandfather crossing a broad desert. Almost without knowing it, he spread the lower pair of barbed wires and slipped through the fence then sat down on the dirt and, all the while letting his imagination expand the story, removed his shoes . He didn't go barefoot much-- he was forever stepping on thistles, and then having to undergo the agony of having his father laboriously dig the thorns out. But he cattle trails were free of thistles-- not even tumbleweeds could withstand the tramp of a hundred cow hooves--and the experience of bare feet in the deep dust was delicious. There still was the hazard of an occasional splatter of cow dung, but that didn't bother him. He'd washed lots of cow manure from his shoes--and from his bare feet.

He tied his shoe laces together with a clumsy knot, strung the shoes around his neck, and stood up. The dog, lying in the shade, raised his head, ears cocked, ready for any adventure the boy could concoct.

"Well, come on, then," the boy said. The dog trotted eagerly to him and nuzzled his hand, and the two of them set off along a dusty trail. Each step raised the dust in a miniature cloud which settled slowly back in the still air. They were a wagon train and every tumbleweed was a forest from which Indians might attack. A startled dusthopper flying away with its wings clacking, became a raiding party in retreat. The green and orange flies burrowing into a day-old "cowpie" were vultures feeding on the carcasses of members of an earlier party, the murders of whom the boy sought to avenge.

Following the crisscrossing trails, lost in his imagination, the boy drifted eastward, and found he had reached the edge of The Swamp. The dog sniffed along, following, perhaps, the scent of pheasant, and entered the edge of the thicket of cattails. "If I'm with him," the boy thought, "I'll be all right," and he followed the dog into the shade of the reeds.

He found trails there, too. The cattle had wandered erratically through the mud, seeking potable water. The boy kept to the hummocks beside the trails, avoiding the mud, which, he imagined, teemed with leeches and other repulsive unknowns. Here was adventure beyond that of the dusty open field, and, though his heart beat stronger, he was unwilling to turn back as long as the dog was with him. They pushed deeper into the maze until, finally, they came to the edge of a pond. Blackbirds stopped singing to scold him. A mudhen dived when it saw him, never reappearing to him but perhaps resurfacing in another opening in the cattails. Standing beside the pond, the boy realized that he had lost his sense of direction and that he didn't know the way out, but he felt no panic at that--he depended on the dog to lead him out.

When he first heard the crashing in the cattails it wasn't really near, but he felt the skin crawl on his neck and arms. *Something* very large was moving in the swamp--moving toward him. Maybe it was the madman he and his friend had created. "Pat," he called sharply. The dog stopped his explorations and looked at him. Now, he too became attentive to the sounds of movement. "Pat," the boy croaked, "*Come here!*" The dog crept over to him and pressed against his legs, tail down, seemingly more frightened than the boy. "Pat, go home!" The dog looked reproachfully at him. "*Go home!*" the boy hissed, not daring to shout and alert the unknown, which, by now, seemed much closer.

He pushed the dog away, and the dog began to slink down a muddy trail, looking back, hopeful that the order might be rescinded. The boy forgot the leeches and the unknowns in the mud, and squished after the dog. The crashing sounds were suddenly near, and he heard water splashing behind him. The dog began to run ahead of him, and the boy, his panic lending him strength and agility he'd never even imagined he had, managed to keep up until the blessed thinning of the cattails showed the safety of the open field.

He ran out perhaps thirty steps onto a dusty path, but his curiosity forced him to turn to confront the menace from The Swamp. Trembling, his heart pounding, his chest heaving, goose-bumps from head to toe, he waited.

He could hear nothing. Only the blackbirds singing and the whine of a single mosquito that had followed him. The swamp was as quiet as if he'd never violated it. The dog coursed about in the edge of the reeds, unconcerned that they had just missed being captured by an unknown horror.

The boy stood still, listening, watching the path from which he'd come, until his breathing eased and his heart slowed. He backed away a few steps, then turned and trotted up the trail toward his house.

The Day the Bus Tipped Over

When I was 10 and 11 years old, we lived about two or two-and-a-half miles from town. I have to admit that I didn't walk 5 miles to school through snow up to my waist when the temperature was 40 below zero. No. I rode a school bus. But there were times when I would have preferred walking.

Our near neighbor, Mr. Snyder, had the school bus contract, and his son, Henry, a high school senior, drove the bus. They lived about a half-mile from us across the field but more than a mile by road. We (my sister Ruth and I) were the third stop for the bus, so we had to ride all the way around the route--six miles or so. It took more than half an hour to get to school in good weather and sometimes an hour-and-a-half in bad weather.

The bus was actually a box built on the back of a 1933 flatbed Ford truck. It was built for utility, not for comfort. The springs were stiff, and if shock absorbers had been invented, nobody around there had heard of them yet. The box had wooden seats and little bitty sliding windows that let in a little air and a lot of dust during the few hot days of early fall and late spring. Imagine fifteen or twenty unwashed (except on Saturday night) children with manure on their shoes, closed into a box maybe eight by fifteen feet on a hot day! We needed all the air we could get.

There was no heat in the bus, except body heat. Even though they were closed in the winter, the windows didn't do much to keep out the drafts and the snow, but we were all dressed for the cold and we hardly noticed it.

Built that way, the bus was really top-heavy. If it were in California now, it would be barred from the freeways even more often than campers and trailers and wind-wagons and other land yachts. All the school buses were built the same way, and there were frequent accidents. It is really surprising there weren't a lot more.

29

Our house was a couple hundred yards or more from the road, down a plain old dirt lane. If we waited at the house whenever it rained or snowed or was foggy, we couldn't see the bus soon enough to run down the lane to catch it, so Dad had fixed us up a "waiting room".

He bought a junked 1926 International truck, made the chassis into a rubber-tired wagon, threw the motor away, and put the cab out by the road as a shelter for us kids. It had all the comforts of home--spiders, drafts, drifting snow, and outside plumbing. That's where Ruth and I waited on bad days, and even sometimes on the pretty days in early May. On the particularly foggy mornings, though, we couldn't see the bus even from our elegant waiting room, and we'd have to go out and stand in the road and hope.

For a ten-year-old, a half-hour on a school bus could be pretty boring. My friend Murdie and I entertained ourselves by flying to school. We were fascinated by airplanes[1]. We nailed one stick (for wings) across another and then nailed on a shorter stick (ailerons). We learned how to carve propellers (and fingers) with our dull jackknives and we nailed our blood-stained, hand-carved propellers to the end of the fuselage. We'd run around with those planes, having imaginary dog fights, sometimes even running fast enough to make the propellers turn, if we ran into the wind. If we sat next to the sliding windows on the bus, we could hold an arm and an airplane out the window (if the bus driver didn't see us) and the propellers turned satisfactorily when the bus got up to cruising speed (25 mph, or so). We even did this on rainy days, whenever the weather wasn't so cold the big kids made us shut the windows.

The day the bus tipped over was rainy and quite cool. Mother took my airplane and told me I couldn't

---

[1]Murdie became a pilot during WWII, was shot down, rescued by French underground, spent 20 years in the Air Force , mostly flying fighters. Murdie died in 1992. I miss him.

have it, because she knew I'd have it out the window and catch cold. When Ruth and I got on the bus, the only other passengers, three boys from up the hill, were sitting at the very back with three egg crates, which meant they had 36 dozen eggs to trade at the grocery store. Such errands were common for the farm kids then. I took a seat by the window, but the air was so cold that I left the window shut and was content to stare out at the rain. When Murdie got on, he mentioned that he too thought the weather was too cold to stick his arm out of the window so he hadn't brought his airplane. Mine wasn't the only mother with forsesight.

The regular bus route was across the top of Ninepipe Reservoir Dam, an earthen dam that shrank from some stupendous height to something like thirty feet over a few years. In my bus-riding days, that dam was terrifyingly high, especially if you were in a top-heavy schoolbus with a driver who was trying to barrel through the muddy ruts so as not to get stuck. And that was on the dry days. On rainy days, the road across the top was slick mud, and the ride across was enough to turn small pagans into saints and whiten their hair at the same time. This day, though, the earnest prayers of the small heathen passengers were answered and Henry decided not to try the dam, but to take the long way around it. Henry's hair was beginning to show some white, too.

We had a long ride that day, over rutted, muddy roads, but we finally picked up the last passenger and were just about a half-mile from the school when the bus gave a lurch, slid into the ditch, and slowly started to lean. All the standing passengers fell over against the lower side, and over the top-heavy old bus went.

Remember, I was first on, and I had a window seat. Suddenly, I was lying with my face pressed against broken glass and grass. The heaviest girl in the whole high school was lying on top of my head, and Lord knows how many kids were on top of her. I was yelling, "Hey, let me up." It seemed like hours before the upper layers climbed out and I could get up. I wasn't the last one out.

31

Remember the eggs? Some of the kids in the back had a right slippery time of it. As they were scrambling out, I remember chanting, over and over, "How many hurt? Anybody killed?"

There were only two real casualties. One girl had a cut in her head, and the last kid on the bus, a boy about my age, had a broken arm, so he ran the couple hundred yards home. We all (except the broken arm) walked, shivering in the rain, the rest of the way to school. Boy did we have a story to tell. Heroes for the day, that's what we were. But then a team of horses ran away in town and our story was forgotten and our glory faded.

We were not to forget, though. For the rest of the school year, every rainy day the bus smelled like old broken eggs, and, as the bus lurched over the muddy roads, conversations died. The only sounds you heard in the bus were knuckles cracking, sweat dripping and an occasional whispered prayer[2], and, sometimes, a unanimous gasp as the bus took an ominous slew.

The next year, Mr. Snyder modernized his bus, streamlined it, lowered the box down to the frame, and even put in a heater. It looked almost like a *real* school bus--until it tipped over.

---

[2] This, of course, was before Madelaine Murray O'Hair, and before the Supreme Court, in its infinite ignorance, forbade such goings-on

Cutting Your Own

To most people nowadays, cutting your own Christmas tree is strictly Dullsville. When we lived in Southern California, Pop put on his scruffy sport shirt and sneakers, Mom tied her hair up and put on a muu-muu, the kids and dog gathered in the station wagon in their shorts and t-shirts, and down the freeway they went to the tree farm. Somewhere along the way, they'd stop at a roadside stand to buy some oranges and grapefruit right off the tree. At the tree farm, they strolled back and forth among the perfectly straight rows, and finally selected "the" perfect tree. The attendant cut the tree, packaged it in nylon net, everybody piled back in the station wagon, away they'd go home, cut the net, and voila'--they'd gone and "cut their own tree". The worst discomfort they were apt to experience was a pebble in a sandal or having to wait for the next exit for a rest stop. Boring!!

Used to be, cutting your own tree could be a real adventure.

The year I was eleven, it looked like we wouldn't have a tree. That was 1936, the year that Mother Nature, hearing that some idiot in Montana wanted a "White Christmas", arranged a good one; on the Thursday a week before Christmas, she dropped just over a foot of snow. Most of the roads were impassable, and some of the school buses didn't get through at all. That didn't make any difference to the School Board. School was *there* and it was up to the student to *get* there.

By Saturday, many of the roads were still closed, and taking a car to the woods the way we usually did was out of the question. As a matter of fact, it had been out of the question since the first freeze, because our car had gone into hibernation and refused to start between the first heavy frost and full leaf of the trees in spring.

If you wish hard enough (and whine loud enough), Fortune will sometimes intervene so your dreams come true. Fortune came in the form of firewood--we were

33

running out. Dad decided he needed to get a load of logs, on the Saturday before Christmas vacation when I'd be home to help saw them into stovewood size. Unlike our car, our horses started in any weather, so he'd take the sled to the woods and trade a sack of potatoes to the resident Indian for the wood. I begged so long and so hard for a tree that Dad finally got mad and gave permission for me to come along and cut one. It sounded like an exciting day to me. Such a trip took a full day, from four in the morning until ten at night. I was so tickled and full of Christmas spirit I even asked my sister if she wanted to go, but she declined gracefully. "You're *crazy*," she said.

I'd forgotten about the cold. When we started out, the temperature was way below zero, and the Northern Lights still played around the whole sky. I rode on the sled on the pile of hay that was to be the horses' lunch, later. It was a lumpy bed but it kept the potatoes from freezing.

Before long the excitement wore off and the cold began to seep in. When my teeth got to chattering so bad the whole sled was shaking, Dad suggested I get off and walk a while. I really didn't want to, but he suggested with the toe of his boot, so I agreed.

Walking behind the sled was a chore because the only tracks in the snow were those of the sled and the horses. I tried to walk the narrow sled track. It wasn't easy, since my farm-boy overshoes were a lot wider than the sled runner, and were so big (so I could grow into them) that I had to take two steps before the overshoe moved. To make sure I got warm, Dad spoke to the horses and they stepped up from a desultory plod to a spirited walk. As the sled pulled away, I began to run and bawl and slip and fall. After what seemed like thirty or forty miles, Dad slowed the horses and let me catch up. I was tired and breathless and *mad as hell*, but I wasn't cold any more. Next time I got off to walk, I held on to the back of the sled.

I looked for a tree while Dad loaded the sled. I think he wanted me out of hearing while he used his

34

verbal English on the logs. Once in a while, when I'd look back, I seemed to see a distinct bluish cast to the air around the sled, but I didn't pay much attention because I was looking up at all the trees around. Besides, I'd already heard that lumberjack lingo.

You'd think that, out in the virgin (well, maybe once or twice) forest, it would be easy to find a Christmas tree. There should be hundreds around, but this one was too big, that one was too short, another turned out to be lop-sided. The one I chose had better be perfect, or my sister would tell me about it all through the Christmas season, and probably through Easter as well. I kept wandering up the hill until I finally found a tree that had a perfect top. It was nearly twenty feet tall, but who cared? In those days, we thought nothing of destroying a big tree for some small part. After all, we cut trees for firewood, didn't we?

When I looked around for the sled, it was nowhere to be seen. In fact, I'd wandered so far away that I couldn't even hear Dad cuss. This was time to practice a little panic, so I tried to do it up right. You may not know this, but when there's a foot of snow on the ground it's hard to run full out in a straight line through heavy brush when you're wearing three pair of overalls and those farm-boy overshoes. I went tearing along at about seven tenths of a mile an hour until suddenly I came upon tracks in the snow. Saved!! I followed the tracks until I came to a place where there was a nice big tree with a good top, then followed them as they went in a straight line through the brush--and came upon another set of tracks. About that time the light dawned, so I followed my tracks back to the sled. I could tell Dad hadn't finished yet--he had a few unused expletives left.

When he reminded me the bleepity-bleep tree was *my* blankety-blank responsibility, I knew it was a good time to be out of the way, so I took the light single-bit axe and went forth. After all, I was an experienced woodsman--I'd watched Dad do it a time or two. I even knew a few appropriate words (which I never planned to use in front of my mother). I took off my mittens to get a

35

good grip on the axe handle and swung away at the tree. That was a twofold mistake. When the axe hit that frozen tree, it bounced off and the vibration came up the handle and stung both hands so badly I screeched in pain and dropped the axe--just before the avalanche of snow from the tree branches hit the back of my neck. I swore terribly--I think I probably even said "darn" and "shucks"--while I dug the snow out of my underwear. I picked up the axe and tried once more, convinced that it couldn't happen again,

It happened again.

Eventually I notched the tree to make it fall away from me, then worked and worried at it until *down it came.* Digging myself out from under that tree, I wished that I had watched Pop a little closer. I also wished I'd kept my mittens. I hacked off what I thought was about six feet of the tree-top and began dragging *my* Christmas tree toward the sled. That's when I learned something new about mountains and foothills. Uphill going doesn't necessarily become downhill coming back. As a matter of fact, when you're dragging something (a tree or a deer, for instance) there sometimes *ain't* no downhill.

Several eons later, when I got back to the sled, Dad was hitching up the horses to start home. I came up puffing triumphantly, dragging *my* tree, inch by inch. Dad looked at the tree, snorted, and with two strokes of his axe cut away a third of what I was dragging. I was horrified and about to bawl, but then he stood up what was left. It was still a foot taller than he was.

We got home early, about nine-thirty, and I rolled my perfect tree off the logs and proudly showed it to my sister. She walked all around it, holding the lantern high.

"That's the ugliest tree we've ever had," she said. "Why, there's a *twig* broken off this side."

She stopped complaining about it around the Fourth of July.

Picking Rock

We were going swimming, my little dog and I. On a hot summer day, I thought nothing could be more attractive than the cool water of the only unpolluted pothole on the farm. Slogging and sweating through a the recently irrigated field, with the steamy odor of wet stubble magnifying the heat, I could think of nothing else. Snooks could, though. She cavorted around me, investigating every movement and smell. Suddenly she ran ahead, her hackles up intent on defending me from the monster she detected hiding in the rock pile.

Rockpiles don't just happen. They are the result of the most odious chore on the farm, picking rock. Rocks left in a field raise Cain with the innards of farm machinery, so farmers pick them up. I suppose that, by now, the process has been mechanized like everything else, but when I was young, the job was done by hand. One of my earliest recollections of working with Dad is of picking rock. I was probably negative in the help scale, so maybe he just wanted company and someone to complain to. Picking rock is a chore that brings out anger and complaint in the most saintly. Especially in a field where there were two rocks for every dirt.

Dad sometimes used a steady team and a stone boat (for you city slickers, that's a platform 8 feet or more long and four feet or more wide on a pair of logs for "runners") and just let the team walk along slowly while he picked along the path of the boat. After I got older, I picked on one side and he picked on the other. Sometimes we used the old Fordson tractor in its slowest gear. It made so much noise we couldn't converse, but our conversation was usually with the rocks anyway. More specifically, with the #@%?**&@%$ rocks. With horses, we could start and stop the boat with giddap and whoa commands. Such commands didn't work with the tractor, maybe because it couldn't hear us over its own noise. Horses stop when they come to a fence, but the tractor had no sense and would barge right on through if we were careless. But, then, the tractor didn't have to be chased down and harnessed every morning.

When the stoneboat got too heavy for the team or tractor to pull, we drove it to the rockpile. The rockpile site was chosen to cover a rock that was too big to dig up, even with a tractor. After a few years, the rockpile in one field was 20 feet across and eight feet high, and I always wondered why the level of the field wasn't lowered when we removed all those rocks from the soil. And why it didn't sag in the middle from the weight of the rockpile.

Different sized rocks took different handling. Some were too small to worry about, so we treated them like undersized fish and threw them back. Minimum keeper was about the size of a baseball and could be handled with one hand. Whether a rock required two hands depended on how strong your back and hands were. For me, a two-hander topped out about the size of a football. Anything larger I tried to roll to the stoneboat. We hitched the horses or the tractor to a rock too large to roll and dragged it to the rockpile. If a rock was too big to drag, some farmers put a stick or two of dynamite under it. Dad didn't fool with dynamite. He just left any rock that big and that's where he built the rockpile. We had several rockpiles in some fields and none in others.

A person would think that once he picked the rock from a field he would be done with it. Not so. Every year the same number of rocks seemed to appear. Some fool advanced the theory that the frost in the winter caused them to heave up. I know better. Those little ones we threw back, like fish, grew into adulthood each year.

A rockpile could be a source of quite a bit of excitement, which shows you how interesting *our* lives were. It was a haven for a species of garter snake, and sometimes for a kind of marmot related to a woodchuck, which we called a rockchuck.

Once Snooks cornered a chuck in the rocks, and got me to clear a path so she could get at it. Then she found out she'd bitten off considerably more than she could chew. That chuck was darn near as big as she was. She fought it for a while, then came running to me and said, "I got him softened up, now you take over awhile." She had a permanently cut lip (and a respect for chucks) after that bout. Oh, by the way. The chuck wasn't very good eating. Better than porcupine, though.

When the ground squirrels (we called them gophers) were just leaving home, they would frequently take temporary refuge in a rock pile. Such was the case on this day. Snooks ran ahead and began whining and snuffling and scratching at a space between rocks. She called me to help her get that varmint out. Between her whines I could hear the whistle of a terrified gopher. I knew it to be a half grown pup, lately ejected from the home by his practical parents, taking refuge in the ready-made catacombs among the rocks.

We held a meeting, Snooks and I, and discussed the situation. I argued for letting the gopher escape this time. I was too hot and too thirsty to spend time trying to evict one little gopher. Snooks, on the other hand, knew her duty and was determined to do it. Even though I argued that we'd have more fun swimming than digging out the gopher, the majority won. I moved the rock Snooks indicated was *the one thing* protecting the gopher. The gopher moved deeper into the pile, and again I moved the *one rock*. Again the gopher moved. Rock by rock I dug for the gopher until I completely dismantled the rockpile, sweating away in the July heat while Snooks pawed at each space and sniffed the delicious odor of quarry. After a couple of hours, I moved an extra heavy rock, and the gopher made a dash for freedom. He didn't find it. In a flash, Snooks had him and he was done for. Snooks, her job done, lay down triumphantly with her kill. I knew that the pain and effort of restoring the pile was far better than the punishment I'd get if Dad found the rocks scattered.

Snooks rested.

Not me. I carried back and repiled each and every rock.

Sleeping in the Cold

When The O'Reilly and I began considering places to live after we retired, she campaigned for the Pacific Northwest. She talked about the changing seasons, the spring flowers and the way the green comes on the trees, the summer showers, and the brisk autumn weather. It sounded pretty good. Then she got to that part about the pristine beauty of a fresh snowfall, and that's when she nearly oversold me. I remembered *sleeping in the cold.*

One of my earliest memories of the joys of sleeping in the cold concerns my bunkhouse experience when I was about ten years old and we lived on the Talbee Place. The Talbee Place? Yes. In Montana, farms were named after their long-time owners, but were never called farms. They were "Places". Why? Heck, I don't know why. Could be it was a holdover from the Midwest, or maybe it goes all the way back to the Pennsylvania Dutch. At any rate, the farm Dad was renting was owned by Sheriff Talbee; ergo, it was the Talbee Place.

Dad was a share-cropper. He supplied the work and Talbee supplied the land, and they shared what little income there was from the crops. One crop Talbee insisted Dad raise (for a few years) was sugar beets. Dad didn't like the sugar beets. He thought they were too much work, and they interfered with his fishing. But Talbee was the owner and he *was* the Sheriff, so Dad had little choice but to go along. They both made a little (*darn* little) money. The stoop labor (and sugar beets need a lot of it) was done by imported workers, sometimes imported from Mexico, sometimes from the Philippine Islands. Ours were usually the latter.

During the beet growing season, "our" Filipinos lived in a bunkhouse. The bunkhouse was a good-sized, one-room shanty, built with a pair of 5- or 6-inch logs under it. The logs acted as skids so that the bunkhouse could be dragged around and repositioned from year to year, depending on where the beet fields were and

41

whether a new outhouse pit needed to be dug. Much of the year, though, the bunkhouse was vacant.

The Talbee house, like most of the farm houses, was the small economy size. I don't remember how many rooms it had, but I do remember that I'd been sharing sleeping space with the dog and two cats in the living room and I wanted out of there and as far away from my sister as I could get. I set out to talk Dad into moving the bunkhouse up close to the house so I could sleep in it. I guess my begger and my whiner were working pretty good. In the late fall, after the sugar beet harvest, Dad cranked up the old tractor and hauled the bunkhouse up to a space between the outhouse and the chicken house just to shut me up.

As usual, Mother put up a fuss, but when I promised to take the dog with me she finally agreed to let me bunk out there, if I wasn't too scared of the dark. I *was* scared. Not of the dark, you understand, but of the lions and tigers and bears and wolves that lurked in it! But I wasn't about to let anyone else know it. Especially my sister.

I had planned to fire up the old pot-bellied stove in the bunkhouse and have my own cozy little home away from home. Well, at least I'd be away from my sister and and the dog would be away from the cats. Those pot-bellied stoves were indestructible and the stove worked all right, but the chimney was only a piece of stovepipe thrust through the roof. I slipped up one day and Mother got wind of my plans, and she hit the roof. She absolutely forbade the fire, saying it was too dangerous. If the bunkhouse caught fire, she said, the chicken house right next to it would burn, too. She didn't want to lose any chickens.

Old Pat (my dog) and I moved out to an unheated bunkhouse. I had cotton sheet blankets and two comforters (quilts, we called 'em) and an old horse blanket that was made of poor quality wool and must have weighed at least 25 pounds. I was warm as soon as I got into bed, although breathing was a bit difficult with the horse blanket and quilts piled on top of me. Getting

42

up, though, was a real *experience* when the weather got a little colder.

My bunkhouse adventure came to an end right after the first real blizzard of the winter. The morning after the blizzard, I found that the snow had drifted against the bunkhouse door and frozen it solidly shut. I couldn't get the door open! I hollered as loud as I could and banged on the door for a while, but no one heard me, so I went back to bed. Fortunately, I had been foresighted enough to bring along a chamber pot. Pat, though, didn't know how to use it, and he suffered a bit. I wasn't in any hurry to be rescued. In fact, I hoped my rescuers would be too late for me to catch the school bus.

When I didn't show up to help with the the milking, Mother came looking for me. By the time she got the ice chipped away and the door open, she was mad as a wet hen, and she gave me holy heck for sleeping out there and then gave Dad what-for for letting me. She moved Pat and me and my horse blanket back into the living room with the cats and my sister. The worst part was, the cats had taken over my bed, and for the rest of the winter I had to sleep in theirs!

When we moved to the Dunbar Place (it didn't become the Hoskins Place until Dad had owned it for several years) one of the first projects Dad began was to expand the house. The house had been as a two-room shack until a bedroom had been cobbled on to make an "ell". We moved into a *three*-room shack. Dad added a porch about eight feet wide across one end and along the North side of the ell. He used the cheapest lumber he could buy--rough cut, green pine. If you aren't familiar with green pine lumber, you may not be aware that it *shrinks*. And *warps*. After a season or two, there were cracks you could--well, no, that's not quite true. You couldn't really throw a cat through them. We tried to cover them with one-by-four boards for batting, but the original boards had warped so badly that there was still enough space to let in good sized mosquitoes during the summer and lots of snow the rest of the year. One section of this new porch on the north side of the house

43

was partitioned off to be my "room", and I slept out there under my quilts and horse blanket. Pat was too old and crippled by rheumatism (and maybe too smart) to join me on the porch.

In really cold weather, I'd heat up a flat-iron, wrap it in a towel, and put it at the foot of the bed. If you've never slept with a flat-iron, I'm here to tell you that an iron in your bed can provoke a lot of anxiety. When you first go to bed, that thing is right off the kitchen range and it's *hot*. As long as it's wrapped in a towel, it's a nice, cozy companion. But after a few nudges with your toes, the towel begins to unwrap, and that exposes the bare iron. When a toe touches that stove-hot iron, the knee-jerk reaction is apt to place parts of your anatomy in the cold, unexplored regions of the bed. It takes a while to locate the warm spots and get everything settled into them again, and to wrap the towel around the iron with your toes. By the time you've got your feet back on the blanketed iron, you're pretty wide awake.

During the night, the iron cools off. Somehow, even though it's inside the warm bed with you, that iron will draw in the cold and be as cold as the outside air. When you turn over in your sleep and touch the bare iron, it's downright hair-raising. This time, you kick the dadblamed iron clear out of the bed, but now it's tricky finding enough warm space to get back to sleep.

Back to the back porch. When the blizzards blew in, the wind found all the cracks. I'd wake up with snow drifted across the bed, in my boots, in my hair (I had hair then), on my pants, everywhere. I'd reach out and shake most of the snow off a sock, snatch it under the blankets and warm it up a bit, put it on, then do the same with the other sock. Then the shirt. So far, not so bad. But next came those heavy, dirty work pants. Young folks nowadays think the work pants we had then were the same then as the Levi's they buy today. Not so. When I was a kid, denim was as stiff as waxed canvas, and when a pair of pants got covered with mud and manure, then froze--well, I didn't want them in bed with me when they were warm, let alone fresh out of a snowdrift, but I had

44

no choice. I jerked those pants on as fast as possible. You might call dressing an eye-opening experience. Sometimes my eyes opened so wide a film of ice would freeze over my eyeballs.

After I dumped the snow out of my boots, I headed for the kitchen. On the rare days I was lucky, Dad had the fire built in the kitchen range. On most days, though, I'd have to build the fire as fast as I could. I'd get the newspaper crumpled, and the kindling laid before I started to shiver. I could even get the wood on top of the kindling, but when I tried to put the stove lid back on, like as not I'd drop it. Did you ever see a fuzzy, blue kid trying to light a fire? The shivering was what made me fuzzy. I'd have made a wino with the morning-afters look like the Rock of Gibraltar. I was worse than old Pat in a thunderstorm. I shook so hard it sometimes took me ten or fifteen matches before I could get a one lighted and into the stove.

I grew up (well, *I* thought I had) and left home, and my maiden Aunt Elsie came to live with the folks. In deference to her city ways, Dad built a real room where the old porch had been, and put in a *bathroom*. A toilet inside the house! We'd always considered that unsanitary!

I went back to visit the old place a number of times before the folks sold out, but I can't for the life of me remember that new bedroom and bathroom. What *I* remember is the old back porch, with the wind howling through, and the snow drifting in, and the feel of the snow when I put those old pants on. Oh, for the good old days!

Ptui!

The Candied Cat

Dowd's mother made cookies. Murdie's mother made cookies. Why didn't my mother make cookies? When I asked her, Mother fussed and fumed and said she was too tired. I had no idea why she should be tired. She only worked half a day in the fields. All she had to do the rest of the time was wash and iron and cook. So what if we didn't have a well or electricity? Didn't I carry in the wood for the cookstove?

"You want cookies, make 'em yourself," she snapped.

And that was that. No offer to help, no advice, nothing. Now that I know more about her earlier life, I wonder if she herself had ever learned to make such sweets.

Though I never told any of my friends of such girlish behavior, I got pretty good at cookie-making. Oh, I had my failures, like the time I mistook the red pepper can for the cinnamon. Those cookies, Dad said, put hair on your chest.

Cookies and even cakes I could handle, but candy was a different situation. My first (and very probably Elroy Blurch's last) experience with candy occurred in the winter of my tenth year.

Elroy lived right across the road, nearer to me than any other kid my age, so we hung around together quite a bit. His mother called him Roy, but we boys called him a lot of things, including "an El of a Blurch." None of us really liked him very much. He was undersized and wore thick glasses and and spoke rather prissily. Besides he was a smart-aleck, and I wanted those honors for myself. El wore jodhpur type corduroy pants and boots that laced to the knee, with a knife pocket on the side. We all made fun of his jodhpurs, but secretly we envied those boots.

The Blurches seemed to be pretty well off. They had a rather large house by local standards; even their outhouse was a three-holer. And they had running water--if you worked the kitchen pump hard enough. I always thought that being the worst thief in the county (which is what Dad thought of Elroy's father) must have paid off well. Mrs. Blurch was well educated and held her head up despite her husband's reputation. She "liked to put on airs", was the way my mother put it.

I liked Mrs Blurch, though. Elroy was one of those people who can turn any situation into a disaster and something went wrong every time we got together. His mother was tolerant and forgiving and I spent a lot of time and got into a lot of trouble at their house

One March day, I had gone to Elroy's house because my mother had insisted that I get out from under foot. We played in the barn for a while, until Mrs. Blurch left to go to town. She called us and told us that, if we got cold, we could go into the house to warm up, but we were to stay in the kitchen. She repeated the instructions several times, making us promise not to go into the rest of the house. I still don't know why. Other than that, she put no restrictions on us. She should have known better, and, in the light of past and future events, should have chained us in the barn.

We very soon got cold. Hunger affected us that way.

Elroy, after surveying the victuals available in the kitchen, lamented that there wasn't anything sweet around. I confided to him that I had made cookies at home, but mother would take a dim view of our going over there for them. Elroy was impressed. I think his craving for sweets made him forget, momentarily, that my confession was a marketable item, subjecting me to blackmail in the future. Of course, he might have realized that blackmailing someone who had less than nothing was--well, blood from a turnip is the cliche.

"Could we make some here?" he asked.

"Where does your mother keep the cookbooks?"

We rifled through the drawers in the kitchen, but the only recipes we could find were a few scraps that his mother kept in a junk drawer.

"Here's a candy recipe. Reckon we could make that?"

I reckoned we could. I forgot, for the moment, that Elroy was another name for disaster.

By the time we got the ingredients assembled and had wiped most of the butter off the table and the door jamb and swept up all but the last half-cup of sugar scattered on the floor, I was beginning to believe in the success of this project.

"Boil the mixture," I read from the recipe.

We fired up the wood stove until it was red hot, and put the pan on to boil. It took only a little while, but by the time the candy began to show signs of bubbling, our faces were as red as the stove.

Elroy's dog, experienced from our adventures, whined to get out, but the big old black and white cat kept rubbing against our legs, purring up a storm, even though we kept kicking her aside to keep from tripping.

When the candy began to boil in earnest it erupted over the edges of the pan in all directions. Elroy, holding the pan handle, reflexively jerked backward, stumbled over the cat, and gyrated wildly to catch his balance. Unfortunately, he kept his grip on to the pan of candy. How such a little panful of candy could cover so much area is a mystery to this day. The cat squalled and left the kitchen so fast she left claw marks on the linoleum floor, and she looked like a dotted line. By the time Elroy regained his balance, the curtains were stuck to the wall, the pan was stuck to the curtains, the spoon was stuck to the pan, Elroy was stuck to the spoon, and I was stuck to Elroy.

Mrs. Blurch chose this moment to return. She walked into the room and stopped. It was not that she was frozen in horror, although she should have been. Her shoes were just stuck tight to the candied floor.

What she said was not at all ladylike. In fact, I sort of wished my dad could have been there. He might have enriched his already extensive vocabulary. The rest of the scene that followed is best left undescribed.

After we got ourselves unstuck and got most of the candy off the floor and the wall and the ceiling (some of it is still there), after Mrs. Blurch's wails of despair died down and after Elroy's wails of anticipation or retribution (that never came) ceased, we became aware of an ongoing wail from the living room. We soon recognized it as the kind of sound a cat makes when it is in deadly peril defending its territory (or making love, but we didn't know that then). We traced the yowls to the space under the living room couch. When Elroy reached in for the cat, she spat at him and refused to come out. From the odor, we could tell we weren't through with our cleanup yet. Finally, we tilted the couch back and found a screeching cat candied firmly to the under side, madder than a wet hen and telling the world about it.

If you have never tried to free an angry cat by soaking candy from its back with the help of an angrier mother, all of you, even the cat, holding your noses with one hand, you just don't know what trouble is.

Screeches and Cream

Before the advent of rural electrification, keeping food cool was a problem for most farmers. Even in the thirties, we didn't have a refrigerator. We didn't even have an ice box, and if we had had one, we had no way to get or keep ice through the summer. Every farm in our area had a root cellar in which potatoes and rutabagas and onions and canned goods and sauerkraut were kept from freezing in the winter. In the summer, the root cellar was cool enough to keep milk from souring for two or three days even in hot weather. Unless, of course, a thunderstorm came through. Everybody knew that thunder soured milk.

On his farm in Iowa, Grandpa had a spring house. Just as the name suggests, this was a little stone building built over a spring where the cool spring water provided a little bit of refrigeration. Grandpa kept his milk in there until the cream rose to the top, then he skimmed off that old Jersey cream, thick as today's ice cream, and ate it on cereal, peaches, strawberries, and even mashed potatoes. Grandpa loved his cream. Cholesterol hadn't been invented yet and, working a farm, Grandpa sure as heck wouldn't have worried about it even if he'd known there was such a thing.

The big problem with the spring house was that it was open, and various varmints found their way in. It wasn't uncommon, in the summer, to strain a few flies and mosquitoes and even an occasional mouse out of the cream. None of those ate very much, so no one worried about them. But when half the cream turned up missing one evening, Grandpa was annoyed. No, that's too mild. He was actually madder than hell, though he'd never say that word.

After he watched for a while, Grandpa saw an old tom cat that hung around the barn slip into the spring house and help himself to the cream. Grandpa drew the line. No goldarn cat deserved cream that Grandpa had reserved for himself. He stuffed the cat into a sack along with some old harness hardware and a couple of big rocks and threw the sack into the Skunk River. When he was rid of that cream stealer he felt much better.

The next day the cat came back and got into the cream again. What really sent Grandpa off was when old Tom came rubbing around his legs and purring. He caught the cat, hit him over the head with a hickory club and threw the carcass over the fence onto the manure pile. Now he was for sure rid of him.

Grandpa should have known better. Cats are notoriously hard to kill, and the next day the cat came back and made off with half the cream again. Grandpa grabbed that cat and beat around on his head until he was sure old Tom was good and dead. Over the fence onto the manure pile again.

The next day the cat came back. By this time, old Tom must have figured he'd had worn out his welcome because he shied away when he saw Grandpa coming. Got his share of cream again, though. Grandpa was madder than ever, so he got out his squirrel rifle and waiting until he could get off a clean shot, blasted the cat good. He threw the carcass over the fence onto the manure pile.

The next day the cat came back. Grandpa figured to use the cat's liking for cream against him. He skimmed off a saucer of cream, put some arsenic in it, and left it in the spring house. Sure enough he came across old Tom in the barn, stretched out stiff and cold. Chortling, Grandpa threw the cat over the fence onto the manure pile.

The next day the cat came back. This time, he ate almost all the cream. Grandpa was livid. He'd drowned the cat, clubbed it, shot it, poisoned it and the dad-blamed thing was still around. This time, he set a trap in the spring house and caught the cream-stealing varmint. He took old Tom out to the chopping block and chopped off his head and threw the pieces over the fence onto the manure pile.

Next day, when the cat came back with his head in his mouth, Grandpa gave up cream.

The Myth

"Looks like he barricaded himself in the old cabin, not that blocking that old busted door would keep anything out," said Ranger Tim Holt. "That's not like Big Jon. He never was afraid of anything in the woods." On the bank of the Big Bear River they found Jon's gun and his pack and his boots, and, scattered about, his clothing. "His clothes aren't torn and there's no sign of blood," Holt went on, poking at the soggy shirt with his toe. "He had his gun out, but it hasn't been fired. Whadda you make of it, Charlie? Think the bears got him?"

"May be," said Ranger Charlie White Cloud. He looked up the valley at the river rolling toward them. "The Old Men of my people tell stories about this place. They say men who come in here turn into bears. That's how the valley got it's name, and why it used to be taboo. They'd say old Jon's turned into a great big bear." He turned and began picking up the scattered clothing. "I figure he cracked his head on a rock and drowned. We may never find him."

Jon Kronik came in from the west, scrambling and sliding along the sketchy deer trail that clung to the side of Big Bear Canyon. He took to the valley floor because he expected easier going, but he was forced to backtrail a dozen times to avoid windfalls and swamps. It was late afternoon before he came out of the forest onto the bank of the Little Bear. He stopped for a moment to let his eyes adjust to the glare, then slid down the gravel bank. The Little Bear wasn't much of a river this time of year. He didn't even get his knees wet when he sloshed across.

Jon shucked his pack in the shade of a willow, and flexed his shoulders to pull his sweaty shirt free. He dropped belly-down at the water's edge and drank noisily, then splashed the icy water over his face and neck and scrubbed at the mosquitoes glued with his own blood to the day-old stubble on his face and the thick black hair on his forearms. He swiped at his face with a much-used red bandanna, then flung it over a willow branch to dry. By the map, he'd come ten miles. Ten miles, hell. Jon guessed he'd hiked more than twice that, and climbed over a thousand feet besides.

A forgotten trapper's ancient cabin stood on the ridge separating the converging Big Bear and Little Bear Rivers. The old-timer had been a good judge of the rivers. Best place to camp was still right there, just a little above the high water mark. Jon picked up his pack and scrambled up the bank to the natural clearing and staked his tent in the cabin yard. He had no objections to a roof over his head but he didn't think much of sharing his sleeping bag with the packrats and other varmints he was sure now claimed the shack. He cleared a campfire space, then lassoed a sapling and hung his plastic bag of supplies high out of the reach of marauding animals.

By the time the sun touched the treetops, Jon was fishing in a riffle within sight of his camp. In a short time he caught his supper, and before the stars were out he'd cooked and eaten the best trout dinner he'd had in months. He sat by the dying campfire watching the dark descend, and listening to his neighbors. A trout splashed in the stream, a nighthawk buzzed an answer from above and something--probably a packrat--rustled and thumped in the shack. He pulled off his boots and scratched at the stumps of his two missing toes. Weather change coming when chilblains itch. If it didn't rain tomorrow, he'd fish the big river for the heavies. He slid into his sleeping bag and dropped off lullabied by the gurgle of the nearby stream and the faint roar of the distant falls where the Big Bear tumbled from the valley to civilization below.

Jon spent the morning hooking, losing and, occasionally, landing the larger trout of the Big Bear. He let them all go. He preferred the smaller ones for eating. Wet to the waist and cold, he returned to his camp at midday and stretched out on the warm sand. A doe and a spike buck crashed out of the brush a hundred yards upstream and, tail flags up, disappeared into the ridge timber so quickly only an experienced eye could have been sure what they were. Jon sat up and scanned the woods across the Little Bear, then shrugged. Maybe they smelled me, he thought, and finished his nap.

Jon was happily playing a trout of respectable size when he became aware of a peculiar odor, making him glance windward. He saw nothing unusual, but he had the distinct feeling that something was watching him. Man, maybe? Nah! A man wouldn't be sneaking around this far from civilization, Bear? Probably not. They're so curious they either come right out in the open or else they panic and light out. Could be a panther, but there were plenty of deer, so any cougar worth his salt should be well fed. Jon decided to blame his imagination and went back to fishing. Nevertheless, before he started supper he slipped his .44 loose from its holster and laid it within easy reach.

After he'd eaten and cleaned up his camp for the night, Jon realized the creepy sensation was gone. Even so, he laid the gun near his head when he went to bed, though he drifted off to sleep almost immediately, too experienced to worry about animals that might be prowling around in the night.

He was bent over his late breakfast fire when something--maybe it was the smell again--made him look up. He almost dropped his frying pan. Sitting on a log across the Little Bear was a huge animal he took, at first, to be the biggest bear he'd ever seen. It was covered with cinnamon-colored hair, but there was nothing bear-like about the creature's position--nor its brown, hairless face, nor its hands.

Jon tried to remember what he'd read and heard about such creatures. There had been newspaper stories about a huge man-like monster of perhaps seven hundred pounds and leaving tracks that gave it the name Bigfoot. Jon had heard about the Indians' man-bear. Sasquatch, some tribes called them. Mythical giants. Yet here one was across the stream from him, not fifty yards away.

Jon Kronik didn't scare easily, but he found himself trembling as he put down the pan and carefully loosened his gun. The creature sat still, just watching curiously. Relieved that his visitor didn't seem hostile, Jon began to relax and think about what he could do. Should he try to leave the valley? The beast was blocking the trail. Not much chance of getting out yet. Well, maybe the thing would just go away.

He thought just going about his business was probably the safest thing to do. Most wild beasts--if wild beast was what this was--ignored you after a while. He took his breakfast dishes and walked slowly toward the stream, not directly toward the monster but angling past so as not to appear menacing. As he squatted by the water scouring his pans with sand, the beast rose and came toward him. Jon stood up suddenly and stumbled back a step. My God, the size.

It was a female. She stood erect, not bowlegged or slouched like an ape. Her shoulders were broad and her chest was huge, and her human-like breasts stood out firm through the hair. Probably young, Jon thought. He knelt to pick up his pans, and the creature came toward him, stopping when he jumped up, as if trying not to alarm him. She wasn't a menace, he decided. She was just curious, so he continued his dishwashing, watching warily as she came closer, studying her face for some expression of intent. Not an ape face. Too much nose, he thought. No forehead, though. Those old-time Indians were right--looks something like a cross between a man and a bear. The size, though. Must be over seven feet. Five, maybe six hundred pounds. She was getting too close. He drew the gun.

"Hello there, young lady", he said. She stopped at the edge of the stream, twenty yards away. "Speak English?" No response, no change of expression. He wished he knew Indian talk. "Look. You stay on your side and I'll stay on mine. Savvy?" Still no evidence of understanding. Jon picked up his equipment and backed, stumbling, toward his tent, watching her

56

intently. She made no move to follow. Presently she went back to her log.

Jon busied himself about his camp, keeping a sharp watch on his visitor. Was she ape or human? Hard to tell. Damn the Indian tales. If he'd never heard them, he could believe she was an ape. What if there were a lot of them? His .44 could stop one, maybe, but not many. Might be better to try to scare her away. Gun in hand, he shouted across at her.

"Get the hell out of here, you she-devil!" The monster scrambled to her feet and shrieked a stream of gibberish. Now he'd done it! He cocked and levelled the gun. The creature shrieked again, looked at him for a moment, then turned and strode away into the woods. Jon breathed again, and sat against a tree as tired as if he'd been running.

Tonight, he'd move into what was left of the shack. He went in reluctantly, and found the place full of spider webs and rat droppings. The roof was mostly gone and the door hung loose. He moved his gear into the cabin, then sought a sturdy pole to bar the door. That would have to do, even if it wasn't very much. The unbelievable myth that had stood there and watched him might return with companions and they'd at least have to make some noise to get at him. He let his mind wander back to civilization. If he told this in town, no one would believe it. Hell, he wouldn't believe it himself.

By evening Jon had relaxed enough to go fishing, though he kept a wary eye on the trail where his visitor had disappeared. Disgusted with his own anxiety, he quit well before dark and returned to camp, cooked his supper and retreated to the cabin early. Tomorrow he'd get the hell out of here.

Jon lay awake for a long time, listening for any sound of movement outside the cabin. Eventually, he slept, and woke from a nightmare, fighting his sleeping bag. Tired and perspiring, he rose and peeked through the cracks in the door, then cursed himself for his timidity. He flung open the flimsy door, and looked across the stream. Nothing. Maybe he'd imagined her?

No, she'd been there all right, but now she was gone. For good, he hoped.

He packed, then decided to bathe away the sweat and fatigue. He crossed the ridge to the Big Bear and, leaving his pack and gun within easy reach he stripped and plunged into a deep pool below a boulder. The sting of the icy water cleared his head and raised his spirits. He scrubbed himself and climbed out shivering and felt it again; he was being watched. He spun round and grabbed for his gun. She stood between him and the trees--how she got there he didn't know. She was so close her estrous odor was overpowering. His cold-stiffened hands were still fumbling with the safety of the gun when she made a movement whose coy suggestion he could not misinterpret. She stretched out her hands, palms up and moved toward him. He watched, fascinated, this giantess performing a dance he'd seen strippers do in Coast burlesque houses, and doing it a damned sight better than any of them. Repelled as he was by her stench and her size, Jon was mesmerized and found himself swaying with her and his naked manhood reacting. By God, he was being seduced! She was very close when he shook off the spell.

"No you don't, gal, he said, surprised at how hoarse he was. "You better stop right there or you're gonna have a couple more holes in you." His voice rose. "Stop, Goddammit, stop!"

He couldn't shoot the woman. He dropped the gun and stepped back, intending to flee into the river, but he slipped, and would have fallen had she not caught him. Huge, irresistible hands seized him and held him easily, gently despite his struggles. She pulled him carefully toward her, as if aware of her overpowering size and strength, and, for the first time, she uttered soft twitterings as she held him close.

For Audrey
(She wanted the story to end.)

This is a valley of singular beauty, where the protective mountain walls rise suddenly from the virgin forest carpet on the valley floor. In the spring, the patchwork of snow and rock on the peaks sparkles in the crisp, clear air. From some peaks, the water of the melt glories in the sunlight and tumbles boisterously over the cliffs to the valley floor. From others, it tiptoes daintily down a series of boulder steps, shaded by a parasol of cedar and fern, scented by the wild rose and mountain laurel. At the foot of the mountains, the waters meet and the Little Bear River is born. This spring when the warm rains flushed the snow from the slopes, the Little Bear awoke and rampaged in its bed, stripping earth and sand and forest fringe from its banks and baring a fifty-yard wide channel of rock and gravel. Nothing survived the onslaught save a few hardy, supple willows that have found room to root among the rocks. In their branches, the flood left its calling card of debris and mud. Flotsam from the spring tide piled against the willows, and below them long clean banks of white sand formed. Now with summer nearly over,the Little Bear flows along sleepily in its bed, then empties into the Big Bear. The willows bloom and prosper, and the sandbars glisten in the sun. On one of the gleaming dunes may be seen a pile of clamshells, and the tracks of a giant, twice the length and breadth of a man's, and spaced a giant stride apart. In close companionship are the bare-foot-prints of a man. Look closely. Two toes are missing from his right foot.

First Date

Your best buddy and long-time pardner should not let you down. When mine did, he let me down with a crash. All because I dated his recent girl friend.

Mickey dated Donna steadily for more than a year, and he figured they had a long time relationship going. But one Saturday night at a country dance, Donna cuddled up close to me and confided that she had decided to break up with Mickey that night. She said he was taking her for granted, and besides, she was bored with him. She said she needed a change.

"Well, " I said, "I guess I'm at least *small* change. Maybe I'll come around then."

"You do that," she said, snuggling closer. She made up my mind right then. She'd see me real soon. Trouble was, she lived twelve miles away, I didn't have transportation, gas was strictly rationed at the time and Dad was very stingy with his car.

A week or so later, Mickey drove over to see me. (We didn't have telephones.) "I've got a date for Thursday night, but she won't go out with me unless it's a double-date. Can you get a date?"

"Sure," I told him confidently, thinking immediately of Donna. "Who's your date?"

"Angie," he said.

I've known Angie since she was a little kid. Angie was a *nice* girl. She had more sense than to date me, but now she intended to go out with my pardner, Mickey. I supposed she probably didn't know as much about him as she did about me.

"Angie!" I said, "Why, she's just a k--uh, she's just a freshman."

"Well, shucks, they all gotta start sometime," Mickey grinned. I guessed that Angie wasn't too dumb, demanding that someone else be along on a date with him.

Came Thursday evening, and Mickey drove up to my house with Angie. "Who's your date?" he asked.

60

"I'll find one," I assured him, voicing a lot more confidence than I felt. Even though Donna had as much as asked me to date her, I hadn't seen her or written her since, and she might have changed her mind. Or been teasing.

Mickey just said, "Hmphh!! Well, you drive."

So I drove. When I pulled up at Donna's house, the look Mickey gave me missed me, fortunately, but it fried a good-sized bush in the front yard.

Donna came to the door in old farm clothes, but still looking sexy as all get out.

"How about a movie tonight?" I panted.

"No, I don't think so," she said. But then she looked out to the road. "Is that Mickey's car?"

"Yup."

Donna thought for about a second, then gave me a smile that had my heart doing cartwheels. "I'll be ready in a minute." And it really didn't take her long.

Now Mickey drove, and Donna sat on my lap, with her arm around me holding me close, especially whenever she thought Mickey was watching.

After the movie and a hamburger at our favorite joint, Mickey drove us back to Donna's. "Hurry up," he said, "Angie has to be home by midnight."

"Okay," I said, but by this time, Donna had begun to take her act seriously, so we stood at her door kissing away like mad. I was not at all anxious to leave.

"Hurry up!!" Mickey hissed from the car.

"Okay. Just a minute."

"Hurry up, or I'm gonna leave you." He was my pardner. I knew he wouldn't leave me, so I didn't hurry. Then he drove away.

Donna was really interested now. She kissed me even harder. "Let's go out to the bus," she whispered. Her father drove a school bus.

I didn't argue. I was too busy trying not to step on my tongue. We got about halfway to the bus, and here came Mickey back, horn honking.

"I'm coming," I called to him, and ran toward the road. Either he didn't hear me, or he was so mad he wanted to punish me. When he drove away this time, he didn't come back.

Donna and I never did get to the bus. All the noise woke up her father.

"Donna! Is that you?"

"Yes, Daddy."

"Better get in the house. Who's that with you?"

"It's Dick. Mickey went off and left him."

"Come on in the house."

He didn't say Donna should come in alone, so I followed her into the kitchen. She made cocoa and we continued where we'd left off, but now the lights were on so our ardor cooled a little bit. No, that's wrong. With Daddy awake on the other side of the wall, it cooled a *lot*-- to barely lukewarm.

After while, I wondered if I'd best be starting home. Donna's dad decided for me.

"Hadn't you better start for home?" he asked, holding the back door open and motioning for Donna to go to bed.

It was a dark and stormy night. Well, actually, the weather wasn't that stormy, but it sure as heck was dark as a dungeon. The clouds were low and heavy so there was no starlight and the night was blacker than the inside of a tomb. To tell the truth, I haven't been inside a dungeon or a tomb lately, but those cliches are as good as any.

I walked along the road stepping in the gravel with one foot and on the grass that grows alongside country roads with the other. For about half a mile. Then my grass foot found--nothing. A ditch under the road ran through a too-short culvert. As I fell, my left side made sudden acquaintance with a large pointed rock, and I thought I'd never breathe again. When I did manage to take a breath to cuss the rock, I wished I hadn't. Taken a breath, that is. Cussing was a necessity. I reached over and poked at spot where the rock had met me. When something grated in there I gave up the investigation.

After a while I gathered up my bones and started off down the road again. Every step and every breath hurt. For the first few miles, I cursed the dark. I cursed the rock that stove in my chest. I cursed Mickey for leaving me, and planned elaborate ways of wreaking revenge. But after a while, I began to think about Donna's warm arms, and how we had almost gone to the bus and what might have happened then. Wow! Daydreams along that line (even at night) pushed the pain into the background. Eventually, either everything went numb or maybe I went to sleep.

A few miles down the road, I caught a glimpse of light and turned to see headlights coming behind me. I knew the only other fool out at that time in the morning had to be the newspaper carrier, and I hoped to hitch a ride with him. Half a mile before he reached me, he turned off to the north and missed me. For the next mile or so I occupied myself cussing him and the newspaper he carried. I do not read the "Missoulian" to this day.

A couple of hundred miles and a couple of hundred years later, just as dawn developed its first cracks, I tip-toed into the house. It did no good to sneak in. Dad heard me anyway.

"Build a fire, Dick," he called out.

To Dad's way of thinking, a feller in good enough condition to stay up all night was in good enough condition to start a full work day.

We built fence. The pain from my rib was bearable, until along about two in the afternoon. When I pulled too hard on the block and tackle wire stretcher, I felt like a mule had kicked me. Dad found me on my knees, cursing and sobbing. I finally told him my sad story. When he heard that Mickey had gone off and left me, that I had walked home from Donna's with what I thought was a broken rib, that the paper carrier had almost given me a ride, his mouth started working like something was pulling on the corners, and he snorted and turned away, his shoulders shaking. He must have been really touched. He even offered to tape my rib, pointing out cheerfully that the tape had to come off sometime, along with all the hair under it. He actually was kind enough to let me sit down for a few minutes. Three hours later I woke up when he called me to help with the milking.

I dated Donna many times after that, but we never did get near that bus again.

Damn!!

Fresh Milk

When our kids were young, every time we drove past a dairy farm and its big piles of manure they'd hold their noses, roll up the car windows, and tell me to drive faster while they complained about the smell. Not me. I sorta like that odor.

It reminds me --

One of the advantages of living on the farm was that we were guaranteed that the milk we drank was strictly fresh. It was so different from the stuff we get today, that's eulogized, traumatized, pasteurized, homogenized, purified, fortified, certified, deified and udderly without character. That's what our milk had--character.

We never kept more than five milch (yes, *milch*) cows that I can remember. Usually we had only two or three. Five was about the most two "men" could milk easily, and I was one of the milkers after I was about 10 or 11 years old. Dad and I each milked two, and the one who finished first had to milk the fifth. Funny, but I was always a slo-o-ow milker.

Farmers who milk cows for profit know that it's absolutely necessary to maintain a morning and evening milking schedule to keep production up. Dad's position was: "I don't want to be tied to the teats of a cow". That would have interfered with his fishing. If you want to get a really early start to be at the stream before daylight, or if the fish are biting and you're an hour and a half from home, you have to decide whether to fish or pull teats. We never really had to make that decision; fishing came first.

Milking cows in the winter has all the charm of a bad case of boils. There are a lot of old jokes about the way cows complain about "Old Icy Fingers." Listen. You don't know what icy fingers are until you've scraped snow off a cow's back with your bare hands when the temperature is down around thirty below. I usually tried to warm my hands up before I started to milk. There's a nice warm place between a cow's bag (that"s "udder" to you city folks) and her thigh, and I'd shove my hands in there until the ice thawed out of them. That was all right for most cows, but we had one or two old prudes that took exception to anyone feeling their thighs and if you weren't careful of their sensitivities, they'd kick you halfway across the barn. Some girls I knew were like that, too.

You might ask why the cows had snow on them. Go ahead!

Well, our milking barn wasn't all that big, and if the cows were kept in at night, the cow--uh--manure piled up and had to be shovelled out every day or so, a kind of work that was against our principles. We had a shed that was supposed to be for all the stock, but the old boss cow never let any of the lower pecking order (cows *peck*?) cows in there. So most of the cows spent the nights in the feedlot, which was deep in cow--uh--manure. When it rained, they came in dripping--manure. Even in below-zero weather, a cow lying on the manure thawed it enough that a great deal of good fertilizer stuck to her. So we had cows with snow on their backs and fertilizer on their bellies. Guess what happened when the cow got in the "warm" barn. Right! The melted snow became water, and the water ran downhill through the--uh--fertilizer and dripped into the milk bucket. That milk had *body*. It had *character*. Not like the tasteless wishy-washy stuff that we get in cartons today.

I miss drinking milk fresh from the cow. Dad and I and the barn cats used to really enjoy it. We kept a tin cup hanging on a nail for us, and an old sardine tin for the cats, and we filled them up and all of us drank fresh, warm, tangy, wholesome milk. In the winter, the cup didn't need to be cleaned--it was in a deep freeze. In the summer the flies kept it clean.

According to the newspapers, the State is still persecuting those dairies that sell raw milk, because it *might* have salmonella in it. Huh!!. The State should have sampled our milk. Salmonella wouldn't have had a chance.

Building Character

Shortly after we remodelled our kitchen, some overly zealous member of the family (I've forgotten who), unfamiliar with the operation of the new kitchen sink faucet, broke the faucet handle right off. Of course, it couldn't have happened while the faucet was turned OFF, so we had people and water running helter-skelter around the kitchen for a while. Someone finally got the taps turned off under the sink, but then there was *no water in the kitchen sink!*

Oh, *tragedy!*

Since The O'Reilly and I both worked at the time, the teenagers did the dishes. Oh, we had a dishwasher, but it was a bureaucrat dishwasher--the right form filled out right, and the dishes pre-rinsed or you got them back the way you submitted them. And it didn't do pans.

67

No water in the kitchen sink! You should have heard the weeping and wailing. I even thought I heard a tooth or two being gnashed. Now, just to rinse a plate, one had to walk *all the way to the laundry tub.* You'd have thought those thirteen steps were up the gallows. After all, a sixteen-year-old who plays soccer at school and lifts weights and runs home for lunch just to keep in shape shouldn't be expected to walk *all the way to the laundry tub* to rinse a plate.

I told the kids to look at the bright side. If the water had been cut off from the dishwasher, too, they would have had to wash *all* the dishes by hand. They looked at me like they were going to be sick , and told me to stop talking dirty.

Now, when I was their age--

The old farm where I grew up didn't even have a pump until after I'd grown up and left home. For years, we dragged the water up from the well in a beat-up bucket at the end of a rope. At first, it was a straight pull, but, eventually, I smartened up and rigged up a squeaky wooden pulley so my sister could get the water.

The bucket was an old galvanized milk-pail that had got too holey to hold milk. It had been banged against the rocks that lined the well until the seams had begun to split, and it leaked so much that we could only get about half a bucket of water to the top, and then you had to be really fast. Dad and I used to brag to each other about it.

"I got a whole half-bucket of water up!"

"Aw, you didn't neither!"

"Well, I got pert-near a half."

The holey bucket sprinkled water all around, and in the really cold weather (we had some of that in Montana) a mound of ice built up around the well pretty rapidly. This, of course, made hauling up a bucket of water even more of a sporting proposition. The hauler had a good chance of joining the bucket if he slipped on the ice, and the higher the mound, the more water leaked out. If a cold snap hung on for very long (and they did) the ice mound got so high that we reached a point of no

68

return. All the water leaked out by the time the bucket got to the top. Then, it was time to get out the axe and hack away the ice or we couldn't get any water at all. As bad as the water in the well was (that's another story!), I don't know, now, why we didn't melt snow for drinking water.

Well, the sink got fixed, and eventually we got back to nearly normal. It took a while. Occasionally, I'd catch someone lovingly stroking the faucet handle. And it was some time before I could mention the "broken sink" without having one or more members of the family run from the room, hand-over-mouth.

Maybe we should get back to basics. Kids ought to have to go out to the outhouse in the ice and snow, and drag water from a well at the end of a rope. Builds up muscles without "exercise". Makes 'em self-reliant. And gives them something to lie about when they get to be old fogies.

Rattler

I never kill a rattlesnake.

Only recently has our general population become concerned with smog and water pollution and their effects on the environment. The fashionable and politically correct have become concerned with the ecological community and the extinction, or potential extinction, of a goodly number of wildlife species. Rachel Carson ("Silent Spring"), J. Frank Dobie ("Voice of the Coyote") and Adolph Murie ("A Naturalist in Alaska") were, many years ago, concerned with and writing about the protection of species and the maintenance of the ecological balance. Perhaps the first alarms were sounded by those personally involved, as was Dobie with the coyote, or those specially trained in ecology, as was Murie. But the usefulness of a generally damned species was demonstrated to me by a particularly spectacular event. My life was saved by a rattlesnake.

Years ago, I was a meat hunter. I was fortunate enough to live in an area in which game and fish were plentiful and provided meat for the table, rather than trophies for the wall. I have since given up hunting and fishing in the wilds and restrict my meat hunting to the more accessible (and economical) aisles of the supermarket.

In my hunting days, it was considered acceptable--even commendable--to destroy, at every opportunity, such varmints as coyotes, rattlesnakes, jackrabbits, ground squirrels, hawks and what have you. Today, it is only with great reluctance that will I take the life of a creature I once considered "fair" game. My personal attitude changed on a day when I hunted moose with the Flathead Indians.

Moose hunting is a con game. The hunter just sits, blowing into his moose call, hoping to imitate the bellow of a love-sick cow moose. The local bull, naturally, slicks down his hair, polishes his hooves, and sets out a-courtin'. And he does not intend for anyone to interfere with his love life.

Don't underestimate the moose. Despite his size and the fact that he is horny (on his head, too) he moves in the woods as quietly as the proverbial mouse. He probably has his reasons. The gentle lady may have another suitor--a big feller--and a bit of surprise on your side never hurts. Or that cow moose with the beautiful voice may be as ugly as--whatever could possibly be ugly to a moose.

It takes years to learn to imitate an amorous moose. First, one must learn what one sounds like, either from the moose herself or from someone who has spent considerable time in her presence. But, with the possible exception of lady moose (meese?) our passionate bull desires few close companions, rivals or no, and to try to associate closely with the lady becomes downright risky. Those who succeed are usually recluse trappers, but occasionally a fortunate hunter learns the song well enough to recognize the imitation when it is well done. If he has the instincts of a confidence man (that is, is human) he becomes one the most respected of con men--a guide.

Knowing the sound made by a lonely lady moose and and imitating it are two different accomplishments.

71

The moose's ear is a well-tuned instrument, and fooling him isn't easy.

I was fortunate. Living on the Flathead Indian Reservation, I had the friendly Flatheads to instruct me. They taught me first what the sound was, and then, amid a great deal of laughter and ribald remarks, how to make it. Eventually, I became good enough that the Indians good-naturedly warned me of the dangers of being raped by a myopic bull.

I was hunting with the Indians in a little valley they call Tih-Se-Soom. I had found a drift log lying between the lake and a small thicket of alder saplings. There I sat and occasionally sounded my moose love call, keeping a close watch for the bull I knew claimed the valley.

I had no results all morning, and was beginning to feel the effects of rising early from a rocky couch. Sleepy, I got careless. Suddenly, he was *there!!* Not nearby--there!! I think I smelled him before I saw him. And when I saw him, I did just what any other experienced, level-headed hunter would do. I ran like heck for the alder thicket, forgetting I had a 30-30 for just this occasion.

The alders were not big enough to climb, but they were big enough to bluff the moose. He stopped at the edge when his huge rack became entangled in the saplings, and began to eliminate them, one by one, scything them down with his antlers. I moved on into the thicket, and then I heard that sound outdoorsmen dread most--the buzz of rattler. In the very center of the thicket, coiled against the base of an alder, lay the biggest Mountain Rattlesnake I ever hope to see. He was not at all pleased by my precipitate entry and he was saying so.

I made an equally precipitate exit through the other side of the thicket.

My friend the moose wasn't so dumb. Realizing I was now outside the thicket again, he came trotting around intending to me severe bodily harm. I decided he was capable of just that. I really had no choice. Back into the thicket.

Mr. Rattler, having had time to become fully awake and to think it over, was in a nasty mood. He struck at me as I went by, intending, no doubt, to teach this young whippersnapper not to disturb the siesta of an aging rattlesnake.

His age was in my favor. Old and large, he was quite slow and I had little difficulty avoiding his strike. I found myself on the original side of the thicket, and, almost immediately, faced by an irate moose. Back into the thicket, past the rattler, to the other side. And, again, the moose.

Back and forth I went, dodging the moose outside the thicket and the rattlesnake inside. Each attempt by the moose reduced the thicket by a sapling or two, and, as the thicket grew thinner, the danger from the rattler increased. Also, I was beginning to tire, and I feared my timing might be a bit slow. Either I'd fail to get into the thicket fast enough and the moose would get me, or I'd fail to get past the rattler. It was the horns of a dilemma--the fangs of a rattlesnake or the horns of a moose.

Youth must be served. Though I was tiring, the elderly rattler was tiring faster, and I began to notice that his aim was poorer each time he struck. I began timing my jumps past him so that I passed close to a sapling as he struck, until, at last, in missing me he struck the base of the sapling.

I kept up my hop-scotch game back and forth, keeping and eye, now, on the sapling. Sure enough, within minutes, that sapling, hardly bigger than my wrist, was swollen until its trunk was a good six inches across, so potent was the snake's venom. As the sap flowed upward, the branches swelled likewise, and shortly I was safely established high in the branches of a tree, making faces at both the rattlesnake and the moose.

Once he could see that I was safely out of his reach, the moose turned away and stalked off toward the lake, stopping at my new rifle to urinate. The rifle never worked again. The snake stayed around the base of the tree for a time, examining the tree, then coiling and repeating the striking action in slow motion, as if

73

wondering how it all could happen. Finally, with a shake of his head and a salute with his rattle, he crawled away, perhaps to consult with his optometrist.

When I was sure they had gone, I climbed down and made my way back to camp, where my hunting companions greeted my story with great glee and disbelief. The next day when I took them to the spot and showed them the drooping, dying alder they had to acknowledge the truth of my tale.

Should you, sometime, find yourself in the valley the Indians call Tih-Se-Soom, look for a grove of alders near the lake. In the center of the grove you may see, now dead and rotting and twisted, a single alder. Treat that tree with respect. That tree--and a rattlesnake-- saved me from a moose.

The Privy

My Aunt Esther (Hoskins) Cheever was born in Iowa in 1900 and grew up on a farm there. She was the youngest of two boys and six girls, whom she often mentioned in her recollections. Many of us who fled the farm get weepy with nostalgia as we recall the joys of the privy, and of the false modesty that the recent generations will not understand. But let Aunt Esther tell about it.

"For private or personal service. That just about covers the subject of the Privy," Aunt Esther said. "For the benefit of those who might confuse it with a toilet, or anyone who might enjoy having his memory jogged, this inconspicuous little building was often called the Out House, or Old Granny Grunts, or Mrs. Jones's, or The Widow's, or the Crappin' Can, or some much less flattering (and less printable) name. One thing was certain--our Privy was *not* a Comfort Station.

"The Privy was always hidden some place in the old orchard next to the yard. Wild mustard (Oh!! The marvelous flavor of spring mustard greens !!), hop vines, and all sorts of berry brambles grew around the scabby old plum trees, and that jungle made a good hideout for the little booth without a telephone. Trumpet vines or morning glories draped over the fence provided good protection from the wandering eyes of anyone passing on the road.

"Once the Privy was moved near Papa's pride and joy--the young Quaking Aspen trees. Another time, it was near the cob house (which made it handy if a man was about--we could go right past him and get an apron full of cobs). There weren't any sidewalks--just boards placed a jump apart and if they were wet, the slightly downhill journey could be hazardous. Wherever the Privy was located, the path led past the woodpile, as all good Privy paths should. If a stranger was in or around the house, it was much less embarrassing to come back to the house with an armload of wood and pretend that was just what we went out for in the first place.

"No paint ever called attention to our Privy, nor did it have moons and stars for ventilation, or lower level seats for small children. If we were short, our legs just dangled, and we leaned forward to keep from falling in. A plain old board served for a lid for those two sharp-edged holes that fit no one. I think the roof always leaked, and a wet seat was gosh-awful cold in chilly November and March. The less said about the blizzards and below-zero weather, the better.

"We kept a warm gray shawl with a deep fringe around it on a nail near the kitchen door so we could make a quick getaway in cold weather. The shawl came with a large safety pin to fasten it under the chin, and was a favorite with all. We suffered a real tragedy when the shawl was lost one cold winter night when Papa took it with him in the sleigh to meet someone at Stark. Even an ad in the Herald didn't bring it back.

"The shawl and a lighted lantern were necessary for night prowling--and oh how I hated to heed nature's call at night. I was scared stiff of the dark and no one ever wanted to go along just for company. I'd call or whistle for the dog, but usually he'd gone out 'among 'em' or was sleeping on the hay in the barn. He'd come to the barn door, decide there was nothing serious wrong, and return to his bed. If Buster, the cat, was around, I'd put him under one arm, but with the lantern in the other hand it was something of a problem to unhook the gate. If I did not have someone with me--even Buster was someone--when I left the privy I backed away a few steps, then ran lickety split. Eerie moonlight was almost worse than a pitch dark night, for there were weird shadows from trees and fences.

"Just before bed time, we sometimes sneaked out only as far as the edge of the porch, but once I was caught in the act when my sister Mabel and her date came walking in the front gate. I didn't hang around them for a long, long time.

"We did use pots, or chambers, for emergencies at night, but whoever used one had to carry it out and nothing was more humiliating than to be seen by a man-

76

-even our own family--when we were carrying a pot. How many hours we must have wasted in agony and dread rather than get up out of a warm bed and go out in the night or suffer the embarrassment of emptying the pot the next morning.

"After the wallpapering was done in the house, any leftover pieces were pasted inside the outhouse. Cartoon pages, colored pages from the seed catalogues and old calendars were added to furnished stimulation for thought when quite a spell of meditation was called for. Once when my sisters were privileged to paste the wallpaper scraps on the privy wall they were feeling especially creative. Mabel would say,

"'Where shall I put this piece ?'

"In the fashion of a tic-tac-toe game, Elsie would say, 'Here'.

"The result was one of the earlier abstracts. Mama's first look at their artistic endeavor brought forth immediate reaction. 'Pshaw! Don't you know how to do *anything?*'

"Another time, possibly inspired by a new baby in the family, the girls cut out all the baby pictures they could find and scattered them all over the walls.

"The mail order catalogue was standard equipment for the privy and we all but memorized it. When it was reduced to only the slick pages, we cleaned out the pattern drawer and saved orange wrappers. Newspapers required considerable crushing and rubbing between the hands to reduce a piece to efficient and endurable softness.

"During freezing weather, we kept a poking stick in the corner. During the summer, we kept lime in a wooden box, and used a small shovel of it after each trip to reduce the odors, and the flies, and the rats. It didn't do much good. The man who first had the idea for a city sewer must have sometime seen a rat swimming in the muck of an outhouse after a rain.

"My oldest sister, Blanche, had children near my age. Milo and I played together almost every day, but there came a time when Mama told me she didn't think

we should go to the privy together any more. We were
too young to get the point although we were willing to
oblige, so each time he had to go he asked me to help
unbutton him and I stood outside and waited until he
came out and then helped put his pants together again.

"The outside door latch was a leather strap and a
nail, and once inside, we took our chances. If we were
two at a time, one could lean against the door, but if we
were alone we had to depend on an extended foot to
partially close the door if we heard heavy footsteps
coming. Of course, the men in our family didn't go near
the privy--that was sissy. It took me some time to realize
that they had the same body functions and need for
elimination that we did, but the evidence around the corn
crib and stud stable finally convinced me. It was much
later that I began to savvy those corn cob jokes that I
heard on the side.

"Preachers, however, made no bones about the
need for such conveniences, and on Sundays we sometimes found a spot behind a bush or in an empty stall in
the barn, for to meet a *preacher* on the Privy path was
just *too much*.

"Monday was privy scrubbing day. We used a
broom and a bucket or two of suds from the washing
machine. On Saturday, we swept the Privy and gave it a
once-over-lightly water treatment if we thought there
might be company on Sunday.

"Despite the cold and snow drifting in the door
during the winter, despite the rain dripping down the
backs of our necks in summer, despite the ever-present
wasps and caterpillars, the Privy was an ideal place to
share a secret or to get acquainted with a cousin. It was
a place to loiter in hopes that someone else would do the
dishes, a good place to bawl when the going got too tough,
and, most of all, a spot for meditation, especially when
the spring morning's sun came through the open door
(for our door always faced east). During a spring thaw,
a feller could sit with elbows on knees and watch the
rivulets running past the door, or throw bits of a broken
stick into the puddle that always formed just outside the

door. It was, after all, a pretty cozy place--for private use or personal service".

The Sears Roebuck Catalogue

Some of us who were raised without the luxury of indoor plumbing regard toilet tissue with a feeling akin to awe. When we "squeeze the Charmin", we do so tenderly and with reverence. Many of us never *saw* toilet tissue until we started school, and some of us not until we were in High School. When we reminisce, we look back fondly to the Sears-Roebuck catalogue and bemoan its passing. The Sears catalogue's dependability and serviceability are the stuff of which folklore is made.

The farm my Dad bought in 1937 had been owned for many years by a man of Scotch ancestry. Mr. Dunbar lived up to the Scotch reputation--he was more than a little bit near. He had not believed it worthwhile to spend the money to really maintain the farm, so the soil was rundown, the fences sagged, and the outbuildings were a mess. Of the outbuildings which he had neglected, the most important was the outhouse (aka the privy). Quite probably the condition of this necessary little hut contributed to Mrs. Dunbar's "sickness", which was their principal reason for selling the farm.

By 1937, the pit under the outhouse was filled up to near ground level. A year or so after we moved in, it was even nearer full. Then came the winter of 1939-40, when the weather was really bad and the temperature went down to below zero and stayed there for weeks. The contents of the pit froze over, and anything that went in froze as soon as it hit the ice down below, so a stalagmite started building. It grew higher day by day, until it reached an alarming height--one who sat down for serious business in the out-house was apt to get more *in* than *out*. It finally became expedient to keep a two-by-four prying bar handy to break off a section of the stalagmite every few days.

Of course, the thaw finally came, and the stalagmite slumped back into the pit, but, by that time, it had become apparent that something had to be done or the effluent would soon reach into the garden.

If you knew Dad, you won't have to be told that he chose to bring up the subject of cleaning the outhouse while we were sitting at the supper table. He winked at me and said: "We won't have to haul it far--we can spread it right there on the garden."

"*You will not* !!!" Mother screeched, before he finished the sentence.

Dad just chuckled and dropped the subject--but not the idea. A few days later, we cleaned the outhouse.

I always hated rubber irrigation boots that were not high enough. I kept getting them full of water, so I bought boots that came halfway up my thighs. These had great advantages--until we cleaned the outhouse. Dad's irrefutable logic--and the toe of his boot--argued that he who wore the highest boots should pitch from the pit. So I did. I got used to the smell after a while, but it sure did hurt my eyes.

We hauled two manure spreader loads from the outhouse and spread them over an old alfalfa field we intended to plow up that spring. After we were done, we parked the manure spreader several hundred yards downwind from the farmstead and hoped for heavy spring rains.

Even in those days, a little packet of radish seeds sold for 10 or 15 cents, which made growing the seed a very profitable business. So, we plowed the freshly fertilized field and planted radishes with the intention of letting them go to seed. Edible crops bear special dividends. When we were irrigating and grew hungry, we could pull up a radish, slosh it around in the irrigation ditch, and have a snack. Those radishes, grown like that in organic fertilizer, were sure good.

Radish seed is harvested much like many crops are harvested now. The dry crop is mowed and rolled into a long windrow which is then picked up by the threshing combine. Our combine had a rubber belt pickup with "fingers" made of heavy spring wire attached to the moving belt. While we were threshing radish seed, we had to stop frequently to pick off the Sears-Roebuck catalogue pages that were impaled on the fingers. It was hard to believe there could be so many-- there must have been twenty years of catalogues.

The radish field was later planted to other crops, the War came along, and I went away, came back, went to college, married and had kids. I was tramping around the farm in 1964, when my eye was attracted to something fluttering on the hog-wire fence that surrounded that field. I went over for a closer look, and found sheets of paper--still recognizable as Sears-Roebuck catalogue pages--caught on the fence.

They just don't build things like they used to.

Winkem

Every Tuesday night, back in the late thirties, we young teenagers of the Methodist Youth Fellowship played a game called "Winkem" under the watchful eye of some of our mothers. It wasn't bundling, but it was as near as we decent Christian children came to that dear, departed custom. Well, in front of our mothers, anyway.

The game required one more boy than girl. If there was a shortage of girls, one of the mothers sat in (Ugh!!). If there was a shortage of boys, a mother took a boys place. (Double Ugh!!) The girls sat in a circle with a boy standing behind each chair, one boy presiding over an empty chair. The guy without a girl winked at a girl of his choice, and she was supposed to leave her chair and go to his. The boy behind her was supposed to try to restrain her. If a boy restrained a girl three times, he had to (got to?) kiss her.

A boy's restraint efforts depended on several factors. If the girl was particularly ugly (or his sister!) or he was too shy to kiss this girl, his restraint might be only a token action, or might be delayed until she got away. If he really *wanted* to kiss her, he made an all-out effort and really grabbed on.

For her part, if the girl liked the boy, she made only token effort to leave him, but if she was shy or disliked him, she'd struggle to get away. This sometimes led to tricky situations. When a boy really wanted to kiss a girl but she was too shy or didn't like him, he tried hard to hold her, and she struggled to get away. Once in a while a dress got ripped or a boy was dragged right over his chair. I'm here to report that *that* was embarrassing, and mighty painful, too.

Or maybe he didn't want to kiss her, but she wanted him to. He'd make token effort and she'd make none. Over time, I was forced to kiss more than one ugly girl, including my best friend's *mother* and my own *sister*.

Couples who were known to be dating frequently were a challenge to the rest of us. If another felllow's girlfriend was in my chair, there was no way I was going let him get her by winking at her. On the other hand, if she were in *his* chair, I could wink all night and not woo her away.

Playing Winkem had one big advantage our mothers did not anticipate. If a guy played his cards-- make that winks--right, he could find out whether he had a chance for a Saturday night date. And Saturday night kisses were a heck of a lot sweeter and more fun than those on Tuesday night, let me tell you.

Best Friend

The boy walked down the lane toward the back pasture, savoring his favorite time of day. The sun had fallen below the dry western hills and eddies of warm and cool air replaced the baking heat of the day. The mosquitoes were out, but had not come down to feast on him yet. He could see the swallows making their last flickering sweeps through the swarms high above the ground. The thump of a bittern (his parents called it a thunder-pumper or, sometimes, by its Indian name, shitepoke) sounded from the swamp nearly half a mile away. The boy's father said that meant rain, but the boy doubted it this time.

The smell of the new-mown hay in the field beside the lane saturated the air. Haying would start in earnest tomorrow, and this year--at fifteen--he'd be expected to do a man's work. He'd draw a man's pay. He straightened up and walked a bit faster.

The little dog ranged far around the boy, joyful now that she was freed from the leash imposed on her during the early days of haying, lest she wander into the path of the mowing machine. She nosed about the hayfield, the delight of the scents registered by the frantic wagging of her stubby tail. A sharp "Yip!" from her bought the boy's attention. A dark, clumsy animal bounded away from the dog, but stopped after only a few leaps. The boy called out sharply. If it was a skunk, the dog had better watch out. The boy climbed through the fence and approached the spot where last he'd seen the animal. A form lurched one jump, and the boy's heart froze.

"Gray." he called. It was his own cat. He could see that two legs had been severed by the mower, and a third hung limp. The cat glared at him without recognition. He was the enemy.

The cat had been his since he was nine years old. That year he had had the measles in late April, and had been incarcerated in a dark room for what had seemed like an eternity. He was forbidden to read or play games or otherwise use his eyes, and the cat, half-grown then, had come in to be his playmate. He had named the cat Gray Baby, later shortened it to Gray Babs and then to Gray. The cat had played under the blankets, and the boy had made up poems and songs. Together they'd whiled away the long imprisonment until the boy had been released one day to the lush, verdant excess of May. That time together had made Gray his best friend.

The boy resisted the impulse to approach the cat as he would normally, to try to pick it up and pet it. He knew that animals that were hurt so badly were not the tame pets they had been, but were wild, unreasoning beasts. He knew too what must be done. The cat was hurt so badly he must be killed, and it was up to the boy to do the killing.

He thought for a moment of his rifle at the house. With the .22, the killing would be easy, but if he took the time to get it the cat might hide some place and die a miserable death. He must do it now. He searched for a weapon, but all he could find was a weathered surveyor's stake. It would have to do. He approached the cat slowly, then struck quickly. A cat's head is nearly indestructible. The flimsy stake shattered, and the cat leapt away.

The boy cursed under his breath, and waited until the cat had settled down again. This time he found a rock the size of his two fists, and then crept up within range and struck. The cat squalled and tried to run, but the boy, losing himself in frenzy, struck again and again and again until the cat's head was a pulp in the mud. The boy found himself kneeling, sobbing, beside the body, the bloody rock held in his two hands. The little dog, shivering in fear, sat apart, watching cautiously.

The boy took off his jacket, lifted the mangled body onto it and carried it to the bank of the big canal. There, where the soil had been dug up and loosened, he dug a trench, using a flat rock and his bare hands. He pulled grass and lined the grave, then laid the cat in gently. Only then did he speak. "Goodbye, Gray Baby," he said. He dragged dirt into the hole, stamped it firm, then brushed over it so that the outline of the grave was invisible.

It was dark, now. The mosquito attack had come and gone without his notice. The cows had long since found their way to the barn. The boy walked back down the lane feeling unbearably spent.

His parents were still at the table, the ruins of supper still before them. They both looked up disapprovingly when he came in, but his mother's anger turned to concern.

"Son!" she said. "What's wrong ?"

The boy was surprised by his own voice--flat, expressionless.

"I had to kill old Gray. Mower got him." His mother started toward him, but his father stopped her. The boy turned and walked out.

Sometimes a man has to cry alone.

H.B.

H. B. Miller owned the farm across the road from ours; he and Mrs. Miller lived in a house that seemed, in the Montana of that time, to be pretty big. It must have been 1200 square feet or so. Even now, I don't know what H. B.'s initials stood for. He had sons named Hillard and Bart, but that doesn't mean anything. It seems to me that the H was for Hiram, but that's just a seem.

H. B. was raised in Kentucky, and homesteaded in the Flathead after mining a while in Butte. He'd raised a pack of kids, all of whom had reputations for being a little wild. When I knew him, he must have been past 60, so his family was grown and all away, but despite his seemingly advanced age, he was as active as a grasshopper, and did more work than most men half his age

H. B. wasn't a recluse, but he wasn't really a sociable cuss either. He was so doggone independent and self-sufficient that he saw no reason to belong to the Grange, and he had no use for organized religion--at least what kinds we had there--so he didn't go to church. He didn't drink, and he didn't socialize at the bars, so he wasn't one of the most well-known of the locals.

I consider myself fortunate that I knew H. B. Miller well. When I was in my teens--just old enough to be doing a man's work--H.B. always called me "Boy" and referred to me as "the boy" to my parents. I never resented it--in fact I was proud that he even recognized me. (When I joined the Navy, he began calling me Dick. I guess he thought I was grown up then.) He was tolerant enough of me that I got special privileges and sometimes I got him to tell me stories he didn't tell just everybody He told me some of the adventures he had, in those early days, when he'd driven a Model T Ford to Spokane--about 200 miles--before there were any real roads. He told about how his favorite riding horse was stolen, too. When I asked what he'd done about that, he told me he saddled another horse and set out after the thief, carrying his Colt .44. He tracked the thief down the valley and up into the mountains above Dixon, but there his story stopped. I wanted to know what happened. The way he looked at me, I wished I hadn't asked. All he said was, "I got m'horse back." It was a while before he told me another story.

Years later I realized that he told his stories with a minimum of obscene words and no profanity. His strongest cuss word was "Dad Blame Me!", and he'd dog- gone or dad blame a jing-bob or a do-ral but never a per- son. H. B. defined a do-ral as that which moves about and a jing-bob as that which just moves to and fro. In times of great stress when tempers were getting short, H. B. was apt to stop, and, apropos of nothing, say, "Don't it beat heck what makes little lizardses?" and then go on working while the rest of us tried to keep from collapsing with laughter.

Dad bought the home place in 1937. He had made the deal and had been around to the banks to try to borrow the necessary money, but in the thirties, bankers tended to welcome a poor dirt farmer looking for money about the way they'd welcome a skunk or a mother-in- law. Especially if he'd been bankrupt once, like Dad had. Getting money from one of them was like riding a buffalo--doggoned near impossible to get started, and pretty rocky once you were aboard. Dad went to the bank in Polson, where he was unknown, with H. B. Miller, who introduced him to the bank president.

"Olsen," H. B. said, "this here's Ernie Hoskins. Better lock up that ole rooster o' yourn. Ernie's the worst chicken thief in these parts. Even got me beat." Then he walked away. What do you say now? Just what Dad said: Nothing.

The banker chuckled. "Well, Mr. Hoskins," he said, "you come pretty highly recommended. If H. B. Miller likes you that much, I reckon we can trust you and do business with you." And he did. Dad not only got all the money he needed, he got extensions of his loans when he needed them, and he did all his banking with that bank until the day he died.

In the late thirties and early forties, we had pheasants everywhere. There were pheasants in the wheat fields, and in the fence-rows and in the cattails by the creek, and in the weeds by the ponds, and even in the orchard right by the house. We who owned the farms considered the pheasants our property--after all, we'd fed them all year--and we resented the city hunters who came out to hunt, although anyone who asked at our house got permission to hunt on our place, if they obeyed the rules--stay away from the house and the stock. Sometimes we'd even go out with them to show them where the best hunting was.

Not H. B., though. He patrolled his place with his .44 strapped on and forbade one and all to come onto his property. He had lost a good work horse once to city hunters, and he had a mad for them forever. Once I witnessed a confrontation between H. B. and some "dudes", and I thought I really was going to see blood shed. When I saw the people stop their car and start through the fence onto his land, I warned them that the owner didn't allow hunting, but they told me that they'd paid their license and that they were going to hunt. They were two men and a woman. One man and the woman had got through the fence when H. B. came up, and said bluntly that they were to get off his land right now. He got some sass. Then the .44 was out, meaning business and it was "Get off my land or I'll shoot you where you stand." The man tore his pants getting back over the fence, but the woman was a little bolder.

"You wouldn't shoot a woman, would you?" she asked.

H. B., raised in the South, was stopped for a second.

"No, ma'am, I wouldn't," he said softly. Then he holstered his 44, picked the woman up, and tossed her over the fence like he would have a sack of grain. His .44 was in his hand before she hit the ground, and the dudes finally decided he meant business and took off. After they'd gone, the funnies hit me, but I didn't dare laugh. H. B. was still fuming, so I kept an indignant face and sympathized with him.

It was a real feather in my cap when he invited me--and only me--to hunt on his farm. Probably it was because he knew how I had been raised: hunt away from the stock, always look before you shoot and don't point a gun at anything you don't intend to shoot. Of course, he might have liked me a little bit, too.

H. B. gave me advice that I'd never have taken from anyone else. When I was 15 or so, I started smoking; it was the grown-up thing to do. H. B. smoked a pipe, but not very often. One day while we were working together in the hayfields, I mentioned to him that I knew I better not smoke in front of my mother, but I wondered about smoking in front of Dad. Dad didn't smoke, but he chewed Copenhagen or Peerless, much to Mother's disgust. H. B.'s response was in his usual indirect way.

"Aw, your Daddy knows you smoke," he said. Then he stopped and leaned on his pitchfork. "I don't smoke very much, you may notice. I used to smoke a lot and I used to drink a quite a bit. We lived in Butte when Hillard was eight or nine, and I always kept a jug of moonshine around and had a few drinks when I came in from the mines. Well, one night I came home and Hillard hadn't split the wood like he was supposed to. I got after him, and he told me to 'Go to Hell, Old Man'. I knew then he'd been at the jug, and was acting like I did after a few. I quit drinking right then." He paused and moved a forkful of hay. "By grannies," he said, "I figure it ain't the best men that don't smoke or drink. It's them that know when to quit."

A man like that makes a lasting impression on a person. Thirty years later my doctor advised me to quit drinking. Well, that's not quite right. What he *really* said was, "You have all the earmarks of a classic drunk!" Right away I thought of H. B. Miller. And I quit. Cold. I sure would like to have H. B. consider me one of the best men.

Nathan

Nathan came to Buck Springs on one of those sunny days in late October when the wind frisks around and you know there'll be a storm soon. I'd just got there myself and was unloading my wagon behind Johnson's place when I noticed a stranger riding down through the trees from the north. Not many came that way. It was a long hard ride from the Blackfoot.

I stopped work to watch him. Hunched up against the cold wind, he looked so small I thought at first he was a kid bundled up in man's clothes, what with that beat-up saddle and that ragged and dirty bedroll. He had a a double-barreled shotgun stuck into the saddle boot where most men carry a rifle. When he rode up to Johnson's hitching rail, I went around to meet him. He swung stiffly from the saddle, and I realized he was no kid, though I'd never try to guess how old he was. Most men's faces get brown out here, but his was nearer gray, and his eyes were about the same color. He didn't just look unhealthy--he looked a lot like a corpse. When he answered my "Howdy!" in a dead-tired voice, it just seemed to fit him.

He flipped his rein around the rail and turned to loose his cinch. I saw his hands stop and his face twitch, and he sort of sagged like something hurt real bad. A look I'd never seen before came into his eyes.

He was staring over the saddle at Bull McGuire who'd just come out of the blacksmith shop. I thought at first it might be Bull's badge, but this stranger didn't look or act like a man on the run. He put his face down on the saddle for a minute, and by the time he looked up again, Bull had gone back into the smithy.

The stranger came up onto the split-log porch and I introduced myself. I hoped he'd ask about Bull McGuire or maybe give some hint of what Bull meant to him, but he didn't.

"I'm Nathan," he said in that dead-tired way. "Any place to bunk up here?"

"Ask inside. Johnson owns about everything you can see except the blacksmith shop. And the shit-house. That's community property."

Nathan didn't even smile. He just looked through me and went on inside.

Buck Springs was like a hundred other gold rush towns I'd hauled freight into for twenty years. When the first strike was made, Old Man Johnson set up a store and a stable and corral and some shacks on the little flat between the hills and the river. I hadn't lied to Nathan; that was about all there was.

Johnson was a bald, ugly, tight-fisted old coot who'd been a miner himself, until he got rheumatism so bad he couldn't take it any more. He'd done a lot better at keeping store than he had at mining. He pretty much controlled the supplies for the fifty or so miners who lived in the cold, muddy tents up in the gulch, scrabbling in the icy water for sixteen hours a day to make half what a man could make at an honest job, but always with that dream of the big strike on their minds and in their talk. Johnson grubstaked them and, when they'd panned out enough gold to pay him, fed them rotgut whiskey till they were broke. Then he grubstaked them again.

Johnson gave a damn for only two things in the world: gold and his half-wit brother. The brother was a huge simpleton, strong as a horse, gentle as a kitten and more animal than man. He looked and walked so much like an upright Grizzly that the miners named him Cub and made him their pet. They teased and loved and protected him, and respected him for the way he got along with animals. Many a miner came down from the gulch with a story about seeing the Cub up there feeding and handling the skittish chipmunks or talking to the crows and camp-robber jays that swarmed around him. One miner even swore he'd spotted the Cub hand-feeding a coyote.

When I finished unloading and started around to settle up with Johnson, Nathan was just heading out to one of the shacks, shuffling along with his head down.

He sure didn't look like the kind who usually shows up in such a Godforsaken place, but then, you never know.

Johnson was picayunish as usual and wrangled about everything on my bill of lading, but finally settled on my terms. What the Hell. He'd make two hundred percent profit on everything I sold him.

By the time we were through arguing, it was too late to start back to Lewistown that night, so I stuck around Johnson's, hoping to hear some yarns. Johnson had set up a split log in the front of the store for a bar, and he had some slab tables and a potbellied stove. The miners came in to thaw out and lie about their pasts and the promise of their claims. Occasionally there'd be a fight about some real or imagined injury, and sometimes somebody'd get cut up pretty bad, or, worse yet, some of Johnson's precious whiskey would be spilled. That's why Bull McGuire wore a badge. The County Seat was twenty miles away, and after Johnson called the Sheriff down twice in two weeks, the Sheriff laid down the law to him.

"Goddammit, Johnson," he said, "the thing to do is stop these guys before they get started. You get these mud-muckers in here and feed them that panther piss you call whiskey and expect to have a Sunday School class. Pick somebody to be your marshal and I'll deputize him. He'll have to crack a few heads, but I won't have to spend half my time coming up here to settle your squabbles."

Bull McGuire was the toughest man around. He'd drifted in and set up a dinky blacksmith shop; he was too lazy to pan gold. Good with a gun and better with his fists, he'd earned his name proving it. Sober, he was rough, inclined to rib a guy pretty badly but with outward good nature. When he was drinking he might be as sweet as your mama's pie, or, if crossed, as mean as a Ma Grizzly Bear. But we'd never seen him what you could call drunk. Nobody really liked him, but then nobody really hated him either. Johnson hoped he could keep peace and keep the liquor supply from being spilled by over-eager combatants.

95

So Bull McGuire became Buck Springs' marshal. He carried the only handgun in town, and kept the peace by knocking heads together whenever he thought it was his duty. Compared to the marshals in some other gold strike towns, he wasn't so bad, either.

I was still trying to put away a glass of Johnson's whiskey when Nathan came in. He'd changed from his dusty trail outfit and even smelled like he'd taken a bath. I invited him to sit down with me so I could get him to talking, but he shook his head and went and stood by the bar and nursed a drink, not speaking to me nor Johnson nor any of the half-dozen miners who drifted in. Nobody paid him much mind except the Cub, who sat behind the bar staring at him the way he usually did a stranger.

When Bull McGuire came in and bawled for a drink, I saw the same look come back to Nathan's eyes. I guess I was watching for it. Johnson introduced them.

"Bull, this is Nathan. Our marshal, Bull McGuire, Nathan."

Bull looked at Nathan for the first time, and jerked stiff. I thought for a second he'd draw, but Nathan wasn't armed, and seemed harmless, I guess. Anyway, Nathan just said, in his dead-tired way, "We've met," and picked up his drink and sat down at a table with his back to the bar.

Bull watched the obvious insult, then shrugged and turned back to the bar and began some serious drinking. Nathan might as well not have been there.

After a while two miners began to argue about why some women were respectable wives and some were whores. It was an old argument--they'd been at it last time I was in Buck Springs. One guy claimed some women *liked* being whores, and chose the life. The other claimed all women wanted a home, and began to tell about whores who'd married and settled down. They got pretty loud before Bull spoke up.

"Balls!" That stopped the argument. "Any woman has a price. Some come cheap and some want your life for it. Some want a wedding ring and a preacher." Bull turned and talked to Nathan's back.

"But if the right stud comes along, he can buy it for pretty words. Right, Nathan?"

We all looked at Nathan, but he just sat there, grayer than ever, staring at the glass he squeezed with both hands.

"Yeah. Ladies and whores, all alike," Bull went on, his eyes still on Nathan. "Once, back east, I knew a *lady*." He spit the word out and washed his mouth with a drink. "Gawd damn, she was beautiful."

Nathan turned around real slow like he couldn't help himself.

"Stop," he said, real soft.

"Real beautiful," said Bull. "She married a storekeeper, and was well off, but she wasn't satisfied with that, was she? She had to have more, and she turned out to be a slut like all the rest."

"You're a liar, " Nathan whispered.

Bull didn't even bother to make a fist. His big open hand sort of wiped up Nathan, chair and all, and splattered him against the wall, where he slid down and lay on the floor hunched up with his hands out toward Bull, as if trying to hold him off. Bull walked over and kicked him. Nathan whined like a beaten dog. Bull laughed and kicked him again. Nathan whined again. Suddenly, the Cub rolled under the bar, wrapped his huge arms around Bull, lifted him up and carried him away, and then stood between him and Nathan. Guess he thought Nathan was some dumb beast to be protected.

Fired-up as he was, Bull threw a half dozen punches at the Cub, drawing blood from his nose, but the Cub didn't move, not even to raise an arm to protect himself. That was too damn much for the miners. They swarmed over Bull, took his gun, pinned his arms, forced him back against the wall. The Cub stood looking at them for a minute, maybe wondering why Bull had hurt him, then he rolled back under the bar and disappeared in the back of the store. When the miners let Bull go he stormed out, swearing, and slammed the door.

Nobody had anything more to say. One by one the miners left; some of them looked at Nathan like they'd like to spit. When they'd all gone, Nathan got up and limped out without a word.

The next morning was a bad one. A blizzard was coming--any damn fool could tell--and I wanted to get going early so I could get through the south pass and onto the downhill trail before the snow got too deep. I shouldn't have much trouble then--the horses would drift with the wind. I saw Nathan's horse saddled and packed beside his shack, so I reckoned I'd have company. The Cub brought out my team. By damn, he sure had a way with animals. They looked like they'd been in a Kentucky stable. Johnson called me into the store.

"Take a message to the Sheriff?" he asked.

"Sure thing," I said.

"Tell him Bull has got to go. If he troubles anybody else here--" his voice trailed off and his Adam's apple bobbed. "Just tell him we need a new marshal, bad."

I knew what he meant. When word got around that Bull beat up the Cub, there'd be lynch talk, then some fool would challenge Bull, marshal's badge or no, and there'd be trouble again.

I had started for the door when, just barely above the whine of the rising wind, we heard:

"McGuire!"

"Son of a bitch!" said Johnson. He grabbed the Winchester from the rack behind him.

Two heavy, spaced shots boomed.

"Shotgun," I said.

Johnson beat me to the door and stopped so suddenly I ran square into him. He eased carefully to the side and set the rifle down, and I could see why. Nathan was up in his saddle with his shotgun laid across the pommel. It wasn't pointed at us, but it sure could be in a helluva hurry. He didn't interfere when we ran over to where McGuire lay face down in the dirt--just kept the shotgun ready.

We knew McGuire was dead when we first saw him, but I guess you always have to look anyway. Johnson rolled him over, then turned and puked into the weeds. One charge had hit Bull in the crotch, and the other had taken away most of his face.

I glanced up at Nathan. He looked different, like you felt when you kissed your first girl. That's the way Nathan looked--like he'd proved something to himself. He turned his horse and rode out the north trail, the way he'd come in. Johnson and I watched him out of sight. The wind was bitter cold now, and a few flakes of snow came riding in on it.

"Man's a damn fool to ride north into a blizzard. He'll never make it to the Blackfoot--horse won't travel against the wind and he'll freeze to death somewhere," I thought out loud. Johnson just nodded.

We never found out if I was right.

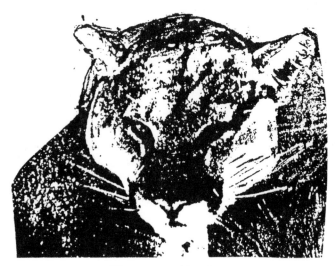

Cougar Bait

My mother was very unreasonable when I was a teenager. Just because I came home from a Future Farmers of America meeting at three in the morning, she denied me the use of the car for a month. I tried to explain that there was this girl, see, and she needed a ride, see, and she needed someone to talk to and that was why I was so late. Mother told me I had used that story before, that she doubted that the girl needed all the comforting she was sure I had given her, and, as a matter of fact, she wondered what kind of girl showed up at a Future Farmers meeting. The more she wondered, the madder she got, and when she threatened to make the restriction last all summer I shut my mouth and high-tailed it to my room (if you could call that cubbyhole a room) making a mental a note to myself to remember, in the future, which excuses I had already used.

Denied the use of a car, I had no hope for any more Future Farmers meetings with the girl, so I was forced to look for other entertainment. My best friend, Mickey, the one who persuaded me to do all those things that got me into the most trouble, lived a mile-and-a-half away. One afternoon, I decided to ride my bicycle over to his house in hopes of relieving the boredom. The fear that one of my classmates might see me on a bicycle was mitigated by the prospect of making more plans for getting into trouble.

The first half mile from my house to Mickey's was gravel road, but the last mile was a rutted dirt road that ran along the bank of a large irrigation ditch, After a rain, it was hard to tell which was the ditch and which was the rutted road. Probably a Conestoga wagon could have gone through, but that road was impassable for any car except maybe a Model T Ford. It was darn near impassable for a bicycle. In some places, I rode along on a knife edge of slippery ground between deep water on one side and the ditch on the other. In other spots, the road was pretty bad.

Mickey and I sat around swapping lies for a while, and one story led to another until finally we got onto the subject of the wild animals that lived in the mountains and occasionally came down into the valley. We told each other all the stories we had heard of encounters with wolverines and grizzly bears and mountain lions, each yarn more hair-raising than the last.

Along about eleven o'clock I realized I should have started home long ago. The night was cloudy and dark as only a Montana night can be. For a moment, I considered asking to stay overnight, but I did not want Mickey to think that his stories had frightened me.

I left the bike at Mickey's, intending to pick it up in a day or two. Riding the bike over that rutted road in the daylight was bad enough but riding in the dark would have been suicidal. Walking wasn't suicidal, merely stupid. Before I had gone a hundred yards, I had stepped into so many water-filled ruts that both shoes were squishy with water. I must have slipped and fallen a half dozen times, and by the time I got to that half mile of gravel road I was wet and muddy and tired and pretty well out of sorts. As a matter of fact, I had long ago run out of cuss words and was inventing new ones as I went along.

The solid footing of the gravel improved my humor, and, since I no longer had to concentrate on keeping my footing, my mind wandered to more pleasant things, such as the stories Mickey and I had told each other. As I was going over a particularly scary cougar story, I thought I heard a rustling in a field alongside the road. I stopped. The only sound I could hear, over the snapping of my hair follicles coming to attention and the thumping of my heart trying to tear its way out of my chest, was a car several miles away.

After a good listen, I walked on. Soon my heart slowed down and some of the hair began to ease down. Then I heard it again. Right beside the road. I stopped, but there was no sound. This time every hair was standing out so stiff I could have made a porcupine hide its face in shame. My heart had long since quit. I listened for a couple of eons and an eternity or two but heard nothing, so I turned my heart back on and started walking again, calling myself several uncomplimentary kinds of coward.

I was only a hundred yards or so from home when an unearthly scream sounded in the field not twenty feet away. That is, the first few microseconds were twenty feet away. The rest just hung in the vacuum where I'd been and never did catch up with me. If you want to break a record for the hundred meter dash, walk along a dark road thinking about mountain lions and have one scream in your ear.

Of course, I knew that couldn't be a mountain lion. Could it? I might have stayed to figure out what other kind of animal made such a horrible sound, but my feet had such a doggone good start it seemed like a shame to waste it.

Between the road and our house was a borrow pit and a five-foot fence. I never was able to jump that fence from the high side, but that night I cleared it from the bottom of that borrow pit without slowing one bit. I did a hook slide in the mud outside the back door, scrabbled into the kitchen and switched on the light. A light in my brain switched on too, and I remembered that H. B. had turned his pigs out into that field along the road. I had heard a pig squeal. Still shaking but satisfied, I went to bed. I left the light on, though.

Next morning, Dad looked at the long gouges in the mud and asked about them. By the smirk on his face, I knew he could tell that a lot of my hair follicles had not yet had time to turn right side out. Since he and his cronies had originated most of those stories that had so conditioned me, I hoped that he might be sympathetic, so I told him the whole story. Hah!! As soon as I was pretty sure he was not going to laugh himself to death, I sneaked away and hid out for the rest of the day. I knew what he'd do--he'd go straight to H. B.

It really hurts when your hero asks, "Hey, Boy. Been et by any o' my cougars lately?" It hurts even worse when he slaps his knee and laughs till he almost falls over. You can't trust anybody.

Fourth of July

When it was all over, Old Jess said, in his usual dry way, "Well, it's the Fourth of July and the boys didn't get to go to the rodeo, so we had one of our own."

In my earliest teen years, Jess Wilson lived on the farm next to us. His granddaughter Bette, the prettiest girl in our school, was about sixteen. She cooked and kept house for him and took care of her crippled grandmother. Her brother Don--but that's another story.

Jess had been a Missouri mule skinner. He usually withheld his mule-skinner vocabulary around Bette and youngsters like Don and me, but there were times when it escaped and when it did, it was educational, to say the least. Mules were uncommon in Montana in the thirties, so Jess bought range horses (Cayuses, he called them) and broke them to harness. His method was to blindfold them, throw on the harness, pull the blindfold and let them try to buck off the harness, while he sat on the corral fence puffing away on his big old chesterfield pipe. When a bronc tired of bucking, Jess caught him up and harnessed him in tandem with Mike, a big gentle white gelding, and put him to work. Between Mike and Jess, the Cayuse would soon learn to work in harness.

Common practice in the depression days was to swap work with men and two-horse teams. Each swapper provided an equal number of man-days and team-days, or, if there was an inequality, one paid the other. The going rate for a man-day was two dollars, and, if I remember correctly, five dollars for a team-day but that included the driver's wages. Dad and Jess swapped work all the time. I don't believe that either ever paid for an unbalance, partly because neither was apt to see two dollars in one piece very often, and if he had, the other would have been embarrassed to accept it.

Dad and Jess both raised a lot of alfalfa hay, and much of their swapped work was in the hay fields. They each had a horse-drawn mower, and a dump rake. They mowed together and raked the hay into windrows, then we (I was big enough to help here) made haycocks out of the windrow with pitchforks. A haycock was ideally just the size a man could pitch in one forkful. When the hay was dry enough, they hired more help for the stacking job.

We had previously raked and "shocked" the hay, and now we pitched those shocks onto a set of slings spread on a hay boat, which resembled a New England stone boat, only bigger. A team of horses pulled each boat, and the driver and a spike pitcher in the field loaded the hay. We stacked using a Mormon haystacker, which was an frame of heavy logs with a long boom pole hung on an A-frame. Pulleys and a steel cable lifted hay up in the slings, which were made to open in the middle. When the hay was where the man on the stack, the stacker, wanted it, someone on the ground jerked a trip rope to open the slings.

To provide power to lift the hay, some crews had the driver of the hay boat unhitch his team, drive around to the pullup cable and hitch to it. This required a person to handle the trip rope, generally a twelve or thirteen year old boy or a farm girl. Another, faster way to provide power was to use a single, steady horse led by that boy (or girl) and have the hay boat driver handle the tripping chore. By the time I was twelve, I was drafted to lead our old, steady mare for pullup on both farms. I was paid a dollar a day, which wasn't bad considering a man's wages were two dollars and found.

Dad and Jess were students of the weather in the Flathead, and they knew that the month of June was almost sure to be rainy up until the 20th or 25th. Some farmers began haying around the 10th of June and almost always got their hay wet. Dad and Jess waited until the weather was sunny after June 20th, and usually after the 25th. Then we had a couple of weeks of haying.

So, as usual, on the Fourth of July we were stacking hay. We had three boats running, two of them drawn by teams of Jess' half-broken Cayuses. I don't know how the first runaway started, but one of the teams took off in the field and ran until they reached a barbed wire fence. Doesn't sound like much, but they ran in a spiral over hay, ditches, whatever, with their driver chasing them and cussing. Dad got a good view from the top of that stack, and laughed so hard he almost fell off. The second runaway started at the stack. A small bundle of hay fell on the backs of the waiting team--Jess' team. This team ran straight ahead for a while, then circled and headed for Jess' barn--on a path that took them between the pullup mare and the stacker. When the hay boat caught on the cable, the old mare leaned into her harness until the cable broke. The runaway team ran right through two barbed wire fences and ended up at Jess' corral.

There was hell to pay. Dad slid down off the stack, and bawled me out like it was my fault the cable got broken, then he and one of the hands set to work splicing it. I believe that they could have welded it with their language. The spot of ground where they worked didn't grow anything for as long as I lived at home.

Jess walked calmly over to his corral, collected his team, and drove them back. At a dead run. "You want to run? Then *run* you @#$%*&!*s," he yelled. And all afternoon they ran, with an empty hayboat or a full hayboat. By evening they were a tired pair of @#$%*&!*s.

By the time we stopped for supper, about sundown, we'd all got over our mads and were able to laugh about the day. What the heck. Not every farm had its own rodeo on the Fourth of July.

Lost

The vast wooded wilderness had been broiled by the noonday sun, and in mid-afternoon lay baking under a lid of steel-gray clouds. The heat had seeped down from the tree tops on the low hills, even to the normally cool banks of the cedar-hidden streams. The whole woodland lay breathless in the hot, dry air.

A burn scarred the wilderness--the wide path of a long ago forest fire lay across the low hills and ended in some distant where. Between the blackened skeletons of fallen giants, crumbling before the onslaught of termite and carpenter ant, the brush once again sprang up. Trailing myrtle and wild grape clung to the ancient stumps, and beside decaying logs, wild roses flourished again. Waist-high buckbrush and Oregon grape grew in self-protective coverts, and here and there a brave young fir tree promised the return of the forest that once was. In the open spaces the cheat grass, its promising lushness of June now turned to dry yellow stems topped with barbed and bearded seed clusters, was spotted by an occasional mullein, with pale-green velvety leaves collaring a tall seed stalk, brown and sere and empty at summer's end.

The cheeky whistle of a ground squirrel, the protective twitter of a field sparrow flushed from its haven, announced the presence of a lone hiker, angling erratically up the slope of a low ridge, avoiding the humps of the rotting trees and the worst of the thorny bushes. A dusty branch caught at his sweat-darkened clothing as if beseeching him to end the summer-long drought. He wished to God he could. As dry as it was, almost anything might start another devastating fire.

The hiker paused to survey the hill above him, and to look back over the valley from which he had come. He passed his makeshift walking-stick to his left hand, then removed his hat and used his sleeve to mop the perspiration from his face and his balding head. The heat itself did not bother him--in fact, he rather relished it--but this stiflingly still air forced him to wrest each breath from the over-heated atmosphere. His heavy khaki clothing, donned against the chill of the early morning and the brookside brambles, seemed to double his exertion. He was glad he had had sense enough to change from rubber boots to sneakers for this hike and to wear his battered hat. He brushed futilely at the swarm of friendly gnats that examined his face, and swatted at the spotted-winged deerfly that buzzed about him, seeking a site from which to pump its meal of blood. At the top of this ridge, he should turn back.

Continuing his climb, he examined the hummingbird's nest in a scrubby bush, the chipmunk burrow under an old tree stump, and the busy bedlam of an anthill. He felt again the nostalgic joy of his youth when he had spent whole days in just such a study, wondering if he'd ever leave the woods. Leave it he had, and now his times of returning were becoming less and less frequent, and consequently more to be savored.

When he reached the top of the ridge he saw before him a forest of big pines--he had reached the edge of the burn. The thought of exploring among those trees and the promised relief from the breathless heat of the burn made him change his mind about turning back. Having come this far, he impulsively decided he must go on.

The big-pine forest was a different world. Suddenly the air was cooler and easier to breathe. The scent of hot dust and buckbrush was replaced by the faint turpentine odor of the pines. The slick, tinder-dry carpet underfoot, woven from needles cast off for decades, lay unmarred by grass, fern or underbrush. He enjoyed the springy feel of it, and, as a proper guest, was careful not to scuff it. The huge trunks appeared to have been, at one time, scrubbed to a bright tan, their patterns then stained by the trickling of sooty rain water. They rose smooth and bare to housetop height, where the lowest limbs, long dead, hung twisted like arthritic hands. He could see deep into the forest through the almost evenly spaced trees, the view becoming indistinct in the distance like a Rubens background.

He wandered far into the forest, contemplating its magnificence. When he sat and rested against one of the pines, he became aware of the enormous silence. Gone were the bothersome insects of the open brush country. No squalling jays, no insistent rapping of woodpeckers; none of the usual forest sounds, not even the sigh of the wind in the pine tops could be heard. He had found real solitude and he was not sure he liked it. He did not know how long he sat in reverie before a needle set, loosened by age, broke from the tree above him and slithered through its kind to become a thread of the carpet below. The avalanche of sound, generally unheard among many others, at once startled and relieved him. The harsh whisper of a distant jet destroyed the sense of solitude as quickly as he had recognized it, and he cursed Man for his intrusion into the wilderness. He must include himself--hadn't he flown his family in here to fish an otherwise inaccessible lake?

He must go back. He had stayed longer than he had intended, so he hurried in a beeline for camp. He was surprised when a deep ravine, the bed of a stream long ago stopped by some geological accident, barred his way. Below him, encouraged by the extra moisture provided by the almost extinct spring, a jungle of ferns and vines entwined about fallen trees. Strange; he must have passed above this point before, and missed the ravine.

Rather than force himself through the mess below, he set out along the edge of the ravine hoping either to skirt it or to find a path through. Presently he found a bridge--a giant pine, undermined in years past until it was eventually windblown across the ravine. It seemed safe enough for a crossing, though he had to work his way among the maze of dead branches. He was almost across when a branch he was holding snapped, leaving him teetering momentarily until he could throw himself prone on the trunk to save himself from a fall to the chaos below.

Excruciating pain tore at his thigh, his chest, his shin. He almost lost his precarious grip on the log as he

109

gasped, too hurt even to curse, for a seeming age, allowing the pain to subside, while he clutched desperately at the horizontal mast. After a time, he pulled himself partially erect, and, somewhat surprised to find no flowing blood and, apparently, no broken bones, he completed the crossing gingerly. Once again on solid ground, he paused to examine the damage done to him by the fall. Through the tear in his shirt, he could see the ugly scratch on his ribs, and he knew the bruise around it would be sore tomorrow. His right shin was scraped blue for its entire length, but his right thigh seemed the most seriously hurt. Some ancient limb stub had done a good job, puncturing deep and injecting the venomous pitch. Lameness was going to be a problem. Mustn't let it stiffen up, he thought. God, he was thirsty.

He had limped, he guessed, about a mile before he tripped awkwardly over a protruding root and pitched forward, this time striking his right kneecap on a rock. He sobbed a curse and in a fury picked up his tormentor-- a two-inch cube of quartz-like stone--and dashed it against another, larger stone. The piece split, revealing yellow threads in a moss-like pattern of peculiar beauty. He stared at it dully for a moment, then excitement gripped him and made him forget his pain. He had seen something like that in a museum. With his pocket knife, he dug out a few of the threads. They came away easily, soft and malleable. Gold! He had discovered gold! The rock outcroppings around him were all of the same quartz. He must be sitting on a gold mine! He shoved the bit of stone into his pocket. How could he mark this place? From here in the deep forest he couldn't see any landmark. He reached for the compass in his emergency kit. The kit was gone, probably torn from his belt when he fell on that damnable log. An uneasiness began to grow within him. He should have been within sight of the lake by now, but he seemed to be far up a hill. Realization struck him like a blow to the heart: Lost!

He resisted stubbornly the impulse to run toward camp. Forcibly rejecting panic, he allowed reason to take over. Obviously his sense of direction, usually accurate, could not be trusted. With no compass, with the sun obscured not only by the pines but by clouds, he *must* act like a man truly lost.

He had always told his sons to *stay put*. Fat chance, with a thirst like this, he thought, and how could anyone find me here without a fire to go by? The old-timers used to climb a tree and look for a landmark. With reason in control, his good humor returned, and the thought of a lame, overweight middle-aged man climbing one of these bare two-hundred-year-old pines framed a ridiculous picture. Was he a cat or something? He almost laughed out loud.

Downhill. Downhill was water, and a man can live for a week with just water. He guessed that he must have a couple of hours of daylight left, and then, if the clouds disappeared after sundown as they usually did, there would be enough moonlight to travel in any country except thick woods. He began working his way downhill among the pines, trying to avoid natural diversions, saving the strength of his weakening leg as much as possible. At times, downhill became hard to define, and he was forced to stop to examine all directions. At such stops, the stillness he had enjoyed such a short time before was disturbingly ominous, reminding him of his predicament.

His mind raced ahead to the oncoming night. If he reached water, he might be rid of the thirst, but at this altitude the night would be cold, and, since he had no matches, he would get little sleep, even if he found a good brush shelter to curl up under.

He wondered what his family would do when he failed to come back by nightfall. They had expected him by mid-afternoon. Sue would be worried now, but by dark she would be frantic, though she would try (unsuccessfully, of course) to hide it from the boys. City-bred, she had never learned to trust the wilds, but had adapted, during their twenty years together, to enduring the inconveniences and insects resignedly, and now rather grudgingly enjoyed camping. "When I show up," he muttered, "I'll catch hell like a kid lost in a department store."

Ted, with the brash confidence of sixteen, would be wanting to search the woods to "see what kind of jam the Old Man's got himself into now." He would be pacing around, hoping to go charging off to become a hero, but restrained by his mother's worried "No!"

He could not predict Dave's reaction. Since graduating from high school, Dave spent his time with an arty (the word was Ted's) group who spoke loudly and bitterly against world conditions and the nation's politicians, though Dave seldom mentioned either. He refused to discuss any of the several scholarships he had been offered, and had come on this vacation trip only reluctantly--he seemed to want to cling to that group of discontents--and, having come, stayed to himself most of the time, admiring his newly acquired beard and sketching the scenes about him.

Should have told them what to do if I failed to show. Never thought of it. Guess I'm just a damn fool who thinks he can't get lost. Dave can fly the plane. What he *should* do is fly out tomorrow morning to get help, taking Ted along to keep him from going off on a wild goose chase, and, of course, taking Sue so she would not be alone. Then if I do get back to camp tomorrow somehow, it'll be deserted. Back to camp? You blamed fool, he chided himself, if you get to water, set up a signal--your undershirt on a sapling or something--and *stay put.* You've been on search parties yourself. You know the guy trying to find himself is the hardest to find.

His musings were interrupted by a sudden awareness of a change in the forest. In the gathering dusk he had not noticed the thinning of the pines. The presence of an occasional stunted fir tree was an unmistakable sign. Even though he was forewarned, coming out of the forest so abruptly surprised him. Suddenly, he stood on a crumbling cliff, the edge of the plateau where the big pines flourished. Below him lay a lake, looking, in the fading light, like every other lake in this wilderness, with its fringes of boggy meadows

112

splotched with aspen groves, and an occasional white fir or cedar stand. At least he could see the sky again, but though the clouds were clearing too few stars were visible to allow him to get his bearings.

The cliff of broken granite, a waterfall in the spring runoff, would have been no appreciable obstacle to him this morning, but by the time he had eased himself down to the rockslides and brush at its base he was sweating profusely, more from the agony of his wounds than exertion. His bruised ribcage rebelled at his panting, and caused him to catch his breath in broken gasps. His thirst-swollen tongue could no longer wet his parched lips. Despite his desperate need for water, he was forced to rest.

"Must be hurt worse than I thought," he mumbled, tenderly feeling his ribs.

After a short rest, he felt ready to tackle the heavy brush. The stiff branches punished him as he forced his way through toward the lake. To his relief, he found a game trail, kept open by the passage of thousands of wild feet seeking the life-giving water. It led him straight to the lake edge, where, belly-down on a flat rock, he buried his face in the water and sucked noisily. Better be careful. A little at a time. Don't drink too much and get a bellyache, too.

His thirst quenched, he lay back against a cedar bole, considering his course for the night. From the corner of his eye, he seemed to see a star at about lake level. He moved around for a better look and there it was--a light! Somebody's camped on this lake too, he thought. Maybe he could get to their camp and, just maybe, they could get word to his family before they did anything rash.

Knowing that the game trail he had found probably encircled the lake, he drew himself up, fought off the pain of his stiffened wounds and sought the trail. If it only stayed low. He knew he could never climb that cliff again even though he had the trail to lead him.

In the deep dusk he could still follow the track easily. The soft damp ground relieved his tired feet, and

113

the ferns and thimbleberry here caressed rather than punished him, so that he felt he was back to the familiar after having been away. He had just turned the corner around a huge stone outcrop when:

"Whuff-f-f!" The snort made his scalp crawl. Bear!

He stood as still as his tormented leg and his terrified heart allowed. The bear stood up among the bushes for a better look. Was this another bear in his territory? In the near darkness, he looked twelve feet high and as formidable as a dragon. For a few seconds man and bear stared at each other, then the man-scent reached the bear and, with snort of distaste, he dropped to all fours and moved away up the slope, avoiding this varmint in his territory as he would a skunk.

The man listened to the animal's movements until the sounds became indistinct. He realized he was holding his breath--he wondered for how long. He exhaled through chattering teeth. It occurred to him that, for the first time that day, he had been scared-- really scared. He made more noise now as he moved along the trail. He wanted to warn the next bear. He knew they usually were dangerous only when they were surprised.

The stars lighted the way--funny how well you can see by starlight--toward the beckoning sign of Man whom he had so recently cursed for despoiling the wilderness, but who now represented hope. If only they don't go to bed early and turn out the light, he thought.

The trail led him through an alder grove where beaver had been working. In the starlight he could see the clean white chips and the pointed stumps that told him there must be a beaver dam nearby. He listened for and followed the sound of water trickling through the dam, and, in a few steps, he had found it. Across its length, high above a scrub fir, hung the light he had sought. Why should anyone hang a light so high on a pole? It was as if they were using the lantern as a beacon for someone they were expecting. Expecting someone? Beaver dam? The universe reeled about him, and

114

suddenly he stood facing a familiar beaver dam, watching his own Coleman lantern. He was home.

If he had not known the beaver dam so well, he could not have traversed it safely with his sore leg, but he moved from log to log with the confidence of many crossings. That effort, the delayed reaction to the bear scare, and his pain made him weary almost to the point of nausea. He wanted to lie down and scream for help, but, by God, he had made it this far, and he could make it the rest of the way on his own.

Another painful hundred yards and he came within sight of the camp, the blaze of civilization under the Coleman lantern.

"Hello, camp," he called.

"Dad?" He saw Ted jump and turn quickly toward him.

"Who'd you expect?" and he struggled toward the light. Seeing his limp, the two sons ran to him.

"What hap--" Ted began, then stopped when his father's warning motion told him not to alarm his mother. "Dad's back, Mom," he called. Sue's voice came from their tent.

"Is that you, Charles? Where on earth have you been? Supper's on the fire if you want it. I'm going to bed." The man grinned. Like a kid in a department store, he thought.

The boys, supporting him on each side, almost carried him to a seat by the fire.

"How'd you get hurt?" whispered Ted.

"Fell on a pine snag. " Their simultaneous quick intake of breath told him they remembered how much it hurt. Dave's fingers were surprisingly efficient as he gently helped remove the torn clothing to expose the wounds. The disinfectant burned like acid,and he swore through gritted teeth as Dave, smiling apologetically, deftly bandaged the ribs and thigh, shrugging at the painful shin. No bandage could help that.

"Were you lost, Dad?" No sarcasm from Ted. Just real interest.

"Let's say I was turned around," he replied.

115

"How'd you find your way back?"

"Came downhill looking for water. I was up in a big Ponderosa forest." He paused, realizing he there was no way to tell them where he had been without retracing his route.

"We were getting pretty concerned," Dave said. "We had a heck of a time with Mom. You know her, imagining all sorts of things, but not saying them and trying to be brave, so we just kept telling her you'd show up for supper." As if in afterthought he said, "I think she's been crying in your tent."

He wolfed the food the boys brought him, only then realizing how hungry he had been. As the boys went about their tasks of securing the camp for the night, their sarcastic bickering excluded him. When they had finished and turned out the Coleman so that the faint glow of the dying campfire was the only light arguing with the darkness, he rose to his feet, found his wounds hurt worse than ever, but limped down to the lake's edge. The stars were close. He listened to the lake lap gently at the shore and watched the moon rise on a beaver's wake.

He remembered the piece of quartz and pulled it from his pocket. In the starlight it was just another stone. He looked around at the dark hills. Up there somewhere was a gold mine. We could cut in a road, he mused, and in his mind he heard the roar and smelled the stink of diesel-driven equipment, chewing ravenously at the earth. Then would come the chain saws and the logging trucks, using the mining road to harvest the lumber for the nation's insatiable appetite. Within months it would all be lost. Lost. He had become rather fond of that word, somehow. It was like a stranger once heard about and only just met and found to be and interesting character.

The boys' steps crunched on the gravel as they joined him. Should he tell them?

"Beautiful, isn't it?" The words from Dave were startling. Dave had been so withdrawn this whole trip that his father had not expected him to voice such sentiment. "Dad, do you suppose it'll last?"

116

"What'll last?"

"This lake, and these woods, and the fishing and-- ah, you know," then he blurted out quickly, "Do you suppose it'll be here in two or three years? Ted and I've been sitting here talking all evening. I guess I'll take that scholarship in England. When I get back in a couple of years, will it still be like this?"

His father rose from his seat and threw the quartz stone far out into the lake. The newly risen moon sprinkled the ripples with silver. A loon laughed its insane call from the distant shore.

"I hope so, Dave," he said.

His leg hurt like hell.

Poor Visibility

Northern Idaho has fog intermittently all winter. Southern California almost always has fog during the months of November and June, and the tule fog in the inland California is known world wide. It seems to me, though, that the fog is not as dense nor does it appear as often as it did twenty years or so ago. Maybe it's because there's less open space now for the fog to sit and brood and grow so nasty and thick that one has to drive the freeway by feeling bumps that separate the lanes, even when sober. But no matter how bad it is now, no fog anywhere--not even that cold, miserable San Francisco stuff--can hold a candle to the fog in the Flathead.

Scientists who are supposed to know about such things claim that the Flathead Valley in Montana is an old lake bed. They say it was part of the lake formed after the last ice age when chunks of ice dammed the flow of what is now the Clark Fork River canyon. As the ice melted the present lake was retained by some rocky hills, but the southern part of the lake drained, exposing the lower end of the valley (Mission Valley) which slopes gradually to the south. This geographical condition gives rise to the phenomenon known as Flathead Fog.

During a Montana winter, everything freezes. Brass monkeys in that part of Montana are all eunuchs. Flathead Lake usually holds out for a while,though. Ice forms around the edges and closes the bays, but there's still open water in the center. The water evaporates to form a fog which boils up over the lake and then drifts southward to the lower valley, where it settles in, and, as the weather gets colder, becomes more and more dense. On a very cold, still day, you can look south from the hills by the lake and see a gray lake of fog, flat as a table, with only an occasional tree or building top showing. The telephone and power poles march down the valley and appear shorter and shorter, until they finally disappear completely in the fog of the lower valley. As you drive south down U.S. 93, the fog rises around the car and you feel much like you are in a submarine, sinking into a gray ocean. It's eerie--you find yourself holding your breath.

Down under the fog, it's twilight. No one drives when the fog is really thick. It's too hard see the road, let alone another car. Even walking can be hazardous. I've been hopelessly lost in a forty acre field that I knew as well as the palm of my hand. I nearly panicked when I came to a fence that I saw every day, but couldn't recognize because my sense of direction had been smothered by the fog. Often, though, even if it's dark at ground level, the fog is only housetop deep, and above the fog the air may be clear all the way to the high clouds.

The winter of '39-'40 was a grim one. Snow and cold came early and by late January the cold really settled in, and so did the fog. Hoarfrost bent the trees to the ground and coated the power lines until we thought they surely would break. The gloomy days became progressively darker and more dismal as the temperature sank and the fog became more dense. And then one morning we woke to total darkness and fog so thick we couldn't see the yard light on the pole fifty feet or so from the house. We had breakfast and waited inside for daylight, but long past what should have been sunup there was still no light. Finally Dad said, "Dick, go out and see what the weather's like." As usual, I objected to being sent out in the cold. As usual, it did no good to complain. Out I went. Oh boy, was it cold! The fog was so thick I had to push it out of the way as I felt my way around in the dark.

Since I knew that the fog often lay only tree-top deep, it seemed like a good idea to see if there was any light at housetop level. I leaned the ladder against the house and climbed up the roof to the ridgepole. When I stood up, I stuck my head through six inches of powdered snow. In every direction as far as I could see, the sun shone on a smooth blanket of white. The fog was so thick the snow couldn't fall through it. I've never seen such fog, not even the tule fog in California. I hope I never do.

119

Lady

When Old Bill Kittmeister came into the cookshack scratched and cut and bleeding and with his clothes all but tore clean off I wondered what the hell had happened to him. He grabbed the bottle of whiskey, took a pull from it, then poured it over some of the worst cuts, cussing through his teeth all the time. I knew him well enough by then to keep from asking any fool questions, but by sorting the wheat of the story from the chaff of his cussing I gathered Old Bill had been in the upper pasture checking his fences when a young she cougar made the mistake of jumping him. Maybe she thought he was a dead deer; that's about what he smelled like.

That young cougar evidently hadn't got all her education or she'd have known better than to tackle a tough old bird like Bill Kittmeister. There must have been quite a fracas; wish I could have seen it. By the time Old Bill got the fool cat hog-tied his clothes were mostly torn off and he was cut and chewed up considerable, but I guess he respected her and sort of felt sorry for her, so he figured that instead of collecting the bounty on her he'd take her down to the ranchhouse and keep her a few days until he had time to turn her loose higher up the mountain where she'd find easier game than old ranchers.

When he carried her over to his horse and went to throw her over his saddle, the bronc didn't share his charity, and went pitching down the trail and took off for the barn. Like I said before, Bill was a stubborn old devil. He'd hog-tied this ninety pounds of she-devil and made his plans for her and, by gawd, he was gonna take her to the ranch. So he walked the five or six miles back to the ranch house carrying the little she-cat, and leaving a thirty-foot wide trail of cuss-burned brush that probably shows to this day. By the time he'd walked all that way, he'd collected a bunch more bites and a few more scratches and lost darn near all the rest of his clothes as well as considerable blood, but he and Lady (that's what

120

he called her) had got pretty well acquainted, and he'd changed his mind about letting her loose.

He kept Lady in the barn and shot venison for her to eat. After a while, she got really big but she was pretty gentle--at least with Bill. No way was *I* going in that barn, though.

Bill Kittmeister looked sixty, but may have been anywhere from forty to eighty. He was a stubborn old coot who gave ground to nobody, even the town bully who out-weighed him by nearly a hundred pounds. Rumor had it that some of his former life wasn't too respectable and that Kittmeister wasn't his real name but nobody had the guts to ask him about it. Guess I was probably the only one around that knew Bill had some funny round, purple, puckered scars on his chest. Fool kid that I was, I wondered out loud about them. Kittmeister's eyes turned real hard and he said quiet like, "Hain't nobody ever learnt ya to mind your own goddam business?"

Mr. Kittmeister (everybody but me called him Bill) had a good-sized spread that started a mile or so below the edge of the timber and reached way back into the patchy woods. He ran a little herd of cattle mostly by himself, doing the cutting and branding himself at roundup, while a neighbor handled the rope. When I was about seventeen or so, I considered myself a pretty good rider and a fair roper and asked if I could ride for him. When I showed him how good I was he said maybe I could flunky around the ranch house, do a lot of the barn chores and cook. He said he hoped I could cook beans a goddam sight better than I could rope cows 'cause if I couldn't we'd both starve to death.

There used to be a lot of troubles in cattle and horse ranching in the foothills on the Flathead Reservation and one of the worst was the deer. Come winter, the heavy snows drove the deer down to the low country and they invaded the ranches and raised hell with the haystacks. The State Game Commission, in its infinite wisdom, set the deer season in the fall before the weather got cold, so the dudes could hunt without freezing their--

without losing various parts of their anatomies. In midwinter, a rancher who defended himself against a herd of deer that was eating him out of house, home and cattle feed risked being stuck with a big fine for shooting game out of season.

Lady kept the deer population down on Kittmeister's ranch that year. When the real winter set in and the deer came down, Bill stopped feeding her and let her hunt for herself. She made a nest on top of the haystack where she waited for the deer and just jumped down on them. After a kill, the hay was safe for a while. Lady lived well during the winter, and come spring when the deer left, she took off to follow the herd.

Bill didn't say much, but I could tell he was heart-broke. He'd played with Lady like he would a housecat, and now he thought he'd never see her again. But one day in the fall, just after the first heavy snows came, Old Bill came in all bleeding and with his clothes tore up and damn if he wasn't pret' near smiling. Lady was back. She took up her old place on top of the stack for the winter.

Before long we were sure that Lady had met up with a Tom cougar during her time away. When spring came and the deer herd moved, she stayed and begged venison from Bill. Her kits were born along about breakup, and Bill was as proud as if he'd sired them himself. There were three of them, and they were kinda cute, even though you chanced a finger if you tried to tickle one of them.

Bill had posted the place, but dudes don't pay much attention to "No Trespassing" signs. One day a feller from town saw there was a cat with a bounty on her and just walked in and shot her. Bill was really busted up about losing Lady that way. He buried Lady (and the dude), under some rocks about a mile up toward the timber.

Now he was stuck with those kits to raise. They were still too small for meat, so Bill figured he'd raise them on cow's milk. Trouble was, we didn't milk cows. For once, I got my back up and told "Mr. Kittmeister" that I was damned if I was going to be a middle-man between a range cow and a passel of lion cubs. Bill gave me a good cussing, but damn near grinned while he did it. Guess he felt the same way. Anyway, he undertook to teach those kittens to suck from a cows tits. Now, if you think the kittens were uneasy about sucking at a cow, you ought to have heard that cow's opinion. She let out a bawl I swear sounded just like a woman's scream, kicked one of the kittens clear across the barn, and tried to tear the whole place apart. She would've, too, but Bill was pretty strong-willed, and cats and cow finally saw the light. One of the prettiest sights I've ever seen was three cougar kittens sitting under that old cow, sucking and purring and trying to see who could get finished first and get the fourth tit.

As the kits grew, of course they followed the cow around, and when they saw her eating grass, they had to try it. It took some time, but those fool cats learned to live on grass just like a cow. Damnedest thing you ever saw-- three mountain lions grazing along with a herd of whiteface cows.

Well, the war came along about then and I joined the Navy. Bill's goodbye was just like him. "Sorta hate to see ya go, even if ya wasn't worth a good goddam around here."

When I finally got back to the Flathead, I went to look Old Bill up, but the ranch was deserted, and the neighbors told me Bill pulled up stakes and left for parts unknown. I thought I might learn something in town, so I went to the local bar. It hadn't changed since I first got thrown out as a snot-nosed kid. Still dark, still sawdust on the floor. Maybe the same sawdust. While I was nursing a beer, a feller staggered in that I could tell had been a good hand before the booze got him. The bartender jumped the bar, put a hammerlock on him, and rushed him back out.

"Crazy son-of-a-bitch," the bartender said. I didn't say anything, but he went on anyway. "Claims he seen some cougars way up in the back country, eatin' grass. Keeps wantin' to tell every outlander that comes in here about it. Figures to get a free drink for it sometimes. Gives my place a bad name."

Like Old Bill learnt me, I minded my own goddam business, and ordered another beer.

Coon Hunt

Little Julie sat on my lap rubbing my head. "Grandpa, I like your shiny head," she said. When you're four years old you can get away with that. "But what are these bumps?"

"Let me look," said twelve-year-old Christopher. "Wow, Grandpa. You've got a bunch of scars up there. Did you get them in the war?"

"No, I got them on a hunting trip," I told him.

The fall I was seventeen, I went to visit my uncle and cousin on a farm in the midwest. Uncle Orrie and Aunt Sophie treated me like royalty, fed me their great big farm meals and put me up on the third floor in an enormous feather bed. My cousin Wayne was younger than I by a couple of years, but he did his best to entertain me. After I'd seen all the stock and the buildings and the harvest, Wayne was running out of ideas. I had the notion that if he introduced me to some of the local farmers' daughters I'd be well entertained, but I guess he didn't think of that.

Uncle Orrie suggested they ought to take me on a raccoon hunt. That way they could teach me about a sport that I could never learn out in Montana. Had I known what was coming, I'd have insisted they let me remain ignorant.

Orrie owned the perfect hunting car. It was an old battered four-door sedan with one headlight and no back seat; the doors were kind of loose and it had no brakes to speak of. That night we piled into the hunting car with a couple of hounds and a kerosene lantern. Orrie drove pell-mell along the narrow, twisty mud road that was scratched out of the cliffs and down to the river bottom where the coon hunt was to start. I sat in the seatless back with a pair of wet coon hounds, alternately praying and holding my breath. This experience was, I felt, truly teaching me a lot already.

I was soon to learn a lot more. I learned that hunting raccoons for sport involves letting the dogs chase the coon while the hunters sit around a smoky fire, coughing and shivering and telling lies until the baying of the hounds says "Treed!" I learned that my Uncle Orrie was a highly principled teetotaller, and could not abide the jug of moonshine or a case of beer most hunters took along. We had nothing to drink but creek water, which wasn't very tasty and didn't warm the innards one bit.

I thought it must be near dawn when the hounds finally treed. Orrie handed me a contraption that looked like an oversized fish net, told me it was a coon net he had designed himself, and that I was to carry it while he carried the lantern and Wayne broke trail through the river bottom brush. Dragging that fool net in the dark through the weeds and hickory brush and brambles was about as easy and entertaining as combing cockleburs off a bobcat. I managed to keep up pretty well, though, and got to the tree about the same time Orrie did. The coon was sitting on a branch making faces and exchanging insults with the dogs. When he saw the lantern and us, he began to get a little nervous, and backed farther out on the branch.

Some folks kill raccoons, and some even eat them, I hear. I hope I never get that hungry. This time, Orrie let it be known that he wanted this one alive to give to friend. Since I was the junior member of the expedition, in experience, anyway, I was elected (not unanimously, you can bet) to shinny up the tree and net that coon. It took a while to get me to the lowest branch since Wayne wasn't very strong and Orrie had the very important (he said) job of keeping an eye on the coon to see that it didn't get away. Where it was going get away to he didn't say.

After considerable sweating, straining and swearing I got up into the tree and crept out on the branch where the coon was. I looked down once, and suddenly realized how high fifteen feet is when you're looking down. The coon hissed at me and backed out farther on the limb. I lay down on the branch, which was starting to bend now, held on with one arm around the branch and swung the net one-handed at the coon.

126

That's when the branch broke. Down came coon catcher, coon net and coon all in a bunch right on top of Orrie and the lantern and the dogs. There was the doggonedest ruckus with more screeching and snarling and snapping and squalling than you ever hope to hear. I guess the coon and the dogs must have been making noise, too. When Wayne got the lantern lit again, the net was over my head, one of the dogs was up a tree, and Orrie had a dog in one hand and the coon by the scruff of the neck in the other. After another tussle, everything settled down, the coon was in a gunny sack and I was spitting out the last of the coon hair. In my opinion, I had had enough schooling for one evening. I was willing to wait a long while for another lesson, but fate had other ideas.

We piled back into the car and started home. The gunny sack full of coon was under my feet in the back non-seat. The dogs were tied to the door handles where they thrashed around complaining that there was a varmint in the car with us and they should be allowed to tangle with it. I had a collar in each hand, holding them off. As we started up the muddy hillside road I felt movement at my feet, and all of a sudden that fool coon was loose. He headed for the high ground--the top of my head. There he dug in with all four feet and held on. Now the dogs really went wild, and they and the coon cursed each other at the top of their voices. Orrie turned around to see what the commotion was and stalled the engine. No brakes, remember? While he tried to start the car, it rolled backward until finally he had sense enough to turn it into the bank. We hit with a thud, the doors popped open and a dog fell out on each side. Just then, Orrie got the car started and drove on up the hill without looking back. The dogs were dragged along by their leashes, but once in a while one or the other got his feet under him, make a lunge for the door and let out a half strangled "Yawp". The coon held the high ground.

At the top of the grade Orrie finally stopped, and he and Wayne jumped out and untangled the dogs. Old Mr. Coon saw his chance and took out for the tall timber,

127

leaving four sets of bleeding tracks to show where he started from. They're still there.

Little Julie sat wide-eyed and fascinated at my story, but Chris looked more than a little bit disappointed.

"Aw, c'mon, Grandpa," he said, "You got 'em in the war, didn't you?"

Valentine Wish

There she comes. She's the one with the flirt in her
     walk,
With the boys clustered round her, and all of them talk
To her hoping she'll favor them with her bright smile
And her laugh that would gladden all Hell for a while.
How can one who's as ugly and worthless as me
Have a hope that a vision as lovely as she
Will give even a smile, let alone her soft touch,
To the one who adores her and needs her so much?
Now her crowd passes by me with nary a glance.
Though I could have called out to her, I missed my
     chance.
Wait a moment; she's stopped and she holds up her hand
Until silence comes over the unruly band,
Then she runs to me, hugs me, and kisses my ear.
"Be my Valentine, Grandpa?" "Forever, my dear."

My Home Town

I left home when I was sixteen, and, for nearly thirty years, when I went back to visit I had to sneak into the valley. The old time residents had made it clear that I wasn't welcome. My exile came about like this.

The committee for the Association of Western Townsites said that, if the town wanted to be classed as an authentic Western town, it had to meet certain qualifications. It had to have, among other things, a mayor to welcome visiting functionaries of various kinds. We elected Windy Harrison mayor, and figured we had it made. Windy had a cleft palate and such a serious speech impediment nobody could understand much of what he had to say. In those days, we said he was tongue-tied, and he was the goat for a lot of the pranks the local boys pulled. When Windy ran for mayor, we couldn't make a lick sense out of his campaign speech, but we concluded that it was the most intelligent and meaningful political speech we'd ever heard. We elected Windy by acclamation.

AWT still refused us.

"In order to qualify as an authentic Western town," the Association representative told us, "you must have a certain set of characters."

"But everybody in town's a character," somebody said.

"No, no. You don't understand. These are special characters. For instance, where's your good-hearted madam? For that matter, where's your whorehouse? Do you have hard working, tobacco chewing blacksmith? You've got a banker, but is he crooked? Where's your marshall? Your bully? There's a whole list of characters you need. Until you have all of these, you don't qualify to join AWT."

When the city father (we were too small to have more than one) looked at the list, he was pretty downhearted. But what few citizens there were rallied around, and nearly everybody took up the challenge.

Oh, we had characters. We had a crooked gambler and a good-hearted saloon keeper and a drunken doctor and so on. But we were such a small town that almost everybody had to take on more than one role. Like they do in Summer Theater, you know.

Take for instance our banker. Seth Goodnight was a relative of the old cattle baron. Seth extended loans indefinitely and did anything he could to keep from foreclosing on a farm. During the hard times, most everybody owed the bank money, but we all kept going because Seth made special arrangements. All in all, he was the required goodhearted banker. On the other hand, Seth turned out to be the lowest of the low-down crooks. He was a *lawyer* and he funded a scholarship for lawyers at Montana State to boot.

Nils Borman was six feet four and 280 pounds. Muscles like iron, strong as a bull. He said he'd take on the job of blacksmith, even took up chewing tobacco. He became the kind of blacksmith Longfellow had in mind, except on Saturday night. Nils walked funny, and on Saturday night he shaved (including his legs) and put on makeup and silk stockings and a wig and a fancy dress and danced with the boys down at the saloon. He even let some of the boys walk him home, but if his escort tried to get too fresh, Nils hit him with his purse. That put one or two of the boys in the hospital.

It was said that, if you looked close on Sandy McGraw's ranch, no two animals had the same brand. And if you looked in his tool shed, you were sure to find tools you'd missed last month. Sandy agreed to take on the job of town marshall, and he made an honest, brave, and determined marshall. Whenever anything turned up missing, the marshall knew just where to look. He'd go fetch the stolen goods, then arrest himself and lock himself up. Some folks worried he'd try to escape, but he never did. He told me he was afraid he might catch himself in the act and have to shoot himself, and he didn't have the nerve to do that.

We didn't have a madam for our whorehouse; didn't even have a whorehouse, for that matter. Sister

130

Superior Agnes from the Indian School offered to act as madam. She set up what passed for a red light district in a few rooms of the boardinghouse. It was said that hers was the best financed school on the reservation.

Pearly Newsome was our pure and perfect schoolteacher. You know, the kind the hero of the old Westerns eventually married. To help out our cause, she worked for Sister Agnes on Friday and Saturday night. Other nights she had to grade papers.

Charley Pope was a clerk at the bank, a quiet, shy little guy. At maybe five feet two and weighing maybe 117 pounds, Charley was the kind of guy you hardly noticed. Since we had to have a town bully, Charley volunteered, and he'd pick a fight with anybody. Got creamed every time. We had no need for a good guy in a white hat to come in and put the bully in his place. Anybody in town could do it.

Every small town had to have an honest storekeeper who sold everything you could ask for--from hairpins to fur coats, from corn plasters to ten-gallon hats, from carpet tacks to John Deere tractors. He was also required to be compassionate and let everybody have credit. John Belchard was our honest, compassionate storekeeper. To fill out the role, John branched out to include opium, heroin, and other peoples' cattle. He got rich repossessing farms.

The Baptist church needed a preacher, preferably one who could preach a rousing sermon on *sin* (the Baptists were against it) and especially on the evils of drink. Arne Jonson volunteered. He was particularly effective when he preached about Demon Rum, since he knew whereof he spoke. Weekdays he was the town drunk, and by Sunday morning he looked (and probably felt) like death warmed over, but his temperance sermons had all the power of honest conviction.

Curley Mitchell took on the job of barber. Curley was our mandatory Mountain Man who came in off his trapline on Wednesdays and Saturdays. He was bald down to his ears, and wore a long full beard. Looked something like an egg sitting on a buffalo robe. Rumor

131

had it that Curley took a bath back in '32, but you couldn't prove it by me. Curley used to sell hair tonic that would raise hair on a smooth rock, and aftershave that would have the girls crawling on their knees after you. Well, that's what Curley *said*.

Dan Sheets ran the garage. Dan could take a tractor or car apart, fix it and put it back together better than new. He never owned a car himself, though. Drove a horse and buggy. Thought automobiles were just a passing fad.

We didn't have enough folks to have a full-time village idiot, so the job was passed around and everybody took a turn. Soon as I was old enough to take my turn, the old timers ran me out of town. They said I just was wasn't qualified.

War

The news came to us Sunday afternoon.
It stunned us by the way the war arrived
Not by our choice, but by other men's.
I'd heard the wise old men say that Japan
Had better watch her step or we might send
Our fleet to sink their islands. Now we had
No fleet.

We listened to reports with private thoughts.
My mother cried and held me close to her.
She said her first love, twenty years before,
Had died in France. She knew what to expect.
My father was a Quaker who despised
All violence, and most of all the war.
His face was sad. He looked at me and sighed.
And I, at sixteen still too young to fight
Hoped fervently the war would only last
Until I too could join so I could grab
Some glory.

When I came home, my glory-reaching hands
Were empty.

Colors

Bald gray heads are bare, hands are on their hearts
Bodies are bent but proud.
The younger ones round them with hats still on
Giggle and comment aloud.

The Unseen Peril

When his son goes away to college, a father usually warns him about the perils to be found on the college campus. He winds up with something like:

"Be good. And if you can't be good, be careful. And if you can't be careful, be sanitary."

None of this does any good, of course, but at least the kid is warned. We really should be more alarmed about the dangers that the boy will encounter that no one has thought to tell him about. I hope I did a better job warning my kids than my father did warning me. At least, I told them about the most fearsome peril of all-- Chemistry lab.

I was a *veteran* when I started college. Why, I was nearly twenty-two years old!! I had not intended to go to college that year. I was planning to take my radio telephone license and ship aboard a freighter for South America. But I ran into my old buddy, Phil, around home. He'd gone to Gonzaga for a year before going into the army, and he sold me on trying it one semester because of all the girls we could meet in Spokane. With that inducement, I decided to humor him.

I went through extensive tech schooling in the Navy, so I was able to take and pass the trigonometry test for credit, but I took the algebra and chemistry classes for fun. I also passed the test for first semester English. At Gonzaga, even Injunears were required to know how to read *and* write, so I enrolled in second semester English. The prof who assigned the subjects for our term papers took one look at me and assigned me the topic, "Contemporary Criticisms of the Contemporary Woman." He recognized a Red-Blooded American boy when he saw one.

The first semester of inorganic chemistry lab was particularly easy. I had done most of the experiments previously. When we were doing quantitative analysis, I dry-labbed all the experiments; I just figured what the results should be and used those answers. I was one of the few in my class who were really acquainted with a slide rule, so even the Teaching Assistants didn't catch on to the technique.

In one of the earliest experiments, we heated potassium chlorate to determine how much oxygen we could drive off. That was a snap to dry-lab. Dry-labbing also produced better than average results, since the potassium chlorate tended to spatter like grease in a skillet, and we usually found that we drove off far more oxygen than the equation showed. So I happily dry-labbed the experiment, and was through in almost no time, then went to help a friend from my home town. Well, he wasn't exactly a friend. He and I had had a girl in common in Montana. And he wasn't exactly from my home town. No matter. I helped him, anyway.

At that time, Gonzaga was a *men's* school. There were no girls in any of the real curricula, but there were some Registered Nurses who were taking credits toward education degrees. But even RN's were female.

There was one nurse in the class who was having trouble with her experiment, so she asked me for help. I found out later she thought I was the lab instructor, and she was after Brownie Points. So I helped her and, after the lab period, invited her to the Gonzaga Canteen for coffee. She was the original Liberated Woman. Remember the term paper? Wow! Great research material! We began by discussing our views. Then we argued. And argued. Finally, one of us--I think she--got mad and walked away. But we met the next week after chemistry lab for another argument. Again, somebody got mad and walked away. I couldn't let it drop, though, because she had the only copy of a book I needed for reference, and I kept trying to borrow it. Something was always in the way, so I got her phone number and kept calling in hopes of finding her in a good enough humor toward me that reminding her would make her bring the book to school.

I could only stand a little of her, and she couldn't stand much of me. So when old buddy Phil asked me to double date with him--insisted, since his girl didn't trust him alone--and my black book came up empty, the nurse was not even to be considered. But Phil was getting panicky--his girl was about to back out--so finally I called the Liberated Woman, expecting (hoping) she'd say no. But she had been stood up that weekend, and was mad enough to do anything, so she said, "OK." There we were, stuck with each other.

That's been forty-odd years, and I still remember the details. We still don't go out together very often, but after raising ten kids, we've got so we don't argue quite so much.

(The O'Reilly saw this and insisted on getting *her* version printed, too. Here it is.)

That's a pack of lies!   Well, anyway he remembers pretty fancifully.

Yes, I *did* think he was a lab assistant. He looked like he knew what he was doing, but I wasn't after Brownie Points, as he so delicately put it. *He could do the math.* He still does the checkbooks--all three of them.

But after the Lab, when we went to talk, I found him to be a really deluded young man. Nowadays, you'd say his head was messed up. He was the epitome of the arrogant male, a Male Chauvinist Pig. As a matter of fact, he still is!

The book he wanted to borrow from me was called "Generation of Vipers", by Philip Wylie. It should have been burned. There was a chapter in it about "Momism", and Wylie said that the American male is dominated by MOM. Whether it's his mother, grandmother, or wife, MOM tells him what to do and what to think. And she takes care of him, so he can run to MOM when his ego gets hurt.

This guy *believed* that stuff!

What I saw was a wild young man with lots of potential going to waste--especially if he quit school and went on that wild goose chase to South America. He needed somebody to look after him.

137

And I was *not* stood up the night of our first date. Tom had called from out of town to say he couldn't get back, so I was free. As for hitting it off--well, by then, we knew each other pretty well from our arguments. When he took me home (on the bus) and asked for a kiss, I told him, "NO!!" Asking for a kiss was sort of expected--the equivalent of the modern "Can I stay all night ?" Anyway, he just shrugged and said, "I'll catch you some other time," and walked away. I was *impressed*. Most guys, you had to fight off.

Well, it turned out the only way to straighten him out was to marry him.

A Sweet Little Nest

There we were, officially committed (or should have been)--we'd set the date. What we needed was a place to live. Our requirements were simple--any little place would do as long as it had two bedrooms, a bath, kitchen and formal dining room, furnished, of course--for what we could afford (i.e., CHEAP). We found all we had in mind (and more) in that old mansion on Spokane, Washington's South Hill. It had a dining room connected to the living room by French doors, and a parlor in front, with a lot of bedrooms and a bathroom upstairs. It even had a "john" off the kitchen (for the servants).

There were drawbacks. For what we could pay, the owner refused to move out or even to get rid of her guests. We, on the other hand, refused the offer of reduced rent in exchange for our domestic service. We compromised. We rented the dining room, kitchen (with the john, remember) and the more-or-less enclosed back porch. The owner would close the French doors and occupy the living room and parlor--with her cats. Unaltered *Tom* cats! We had access to the back (servants') stairs so we could get to the bathroom upstairs. The paying guests occupied the upstairs, including, most of the time, the bathroom.

We never knew exactly how many roomers there were, but we detected at least two male voices singing some song that went "Rome me over under clover", or something like that. The O'Reilly said the words were dirty and I was too young to hear them.

I moved in a month or so before the wedding. This had several advantages--I no longer lived clear across town (must have been three miles) so it was easier to get together. And it had privacy. If you need to hear more advantages than those, you're too darn young to be reading this.

Spokane's buses stopped running at 1:00 AM. No, that's inaccurate--I don't mean they all ran down like

139

clocks. Actually, the buses all went through downtown, and the last bus on each line left downtown at 1:00 AM. Now, is that better? You can see the disadvantage this presented for a young man courting. (If you can't, you're reading the wrong book.) The last time this schedule was a distinct disadvantage to me was the night of my bachelor party. I can see it all now as clearly as I could that night all those years ago. Perhaps more clearly.

We had a little over a week left. We were scheduled to go to Potlatch, Idaho (The O'Reilly's home) for the weekend, mid-term exams were the next week, and then the wedding was the following weekend. My friends chose a Thursday night for the bachelor party. Never mind that we all had school the next day--what the heck, we were all young then. So a few of the guys chipped in and bought a bottle of expensive whiskey (I think it was Four Roses or Three Feathers, or Two Bucks or something) and came over to my new place. We had a really wild and crazy time--played penny ante poker,which none of us could afford, until time for the guys to catch the last bus. About two fingers of whiskey still remained in the bottle. My friends all said, "Drink it. We aren't leaving until it's all gone." I was tired, and besides, I certainly didn't want them to miss the *last bus*. So I drank it. *All* of it. Guzzled it is a better word. After a short discussion about whether I'd choke to death and whether that much whiskey all at once would kill me, they all left. I went to bed. That was my first mistake.

Right away, that bed began to give me trouble. I was lying perfectly still, but the bed wasn't. Pretty soon, I decided that, if the bed wouldn't behave, we'd better part company. So I rolled out and the floor came right out of nowhere and hit me up alongside the head. The blankety blank floor wouldn't stay still either, and I began to feel a need to visit the john. Trouble was, every time I looked, the john was in a different place. I wasn't feeling too good by the time I made contact--must have been something I ate. I vaguely remembered the argument my friends had regarding the fatality of that

140

much whiskey. For a while it looked like the "Ayes" had it, and then it got so I was voting with them.

About dawn I dragged what was left of me (mere skin and bones--anything loose had long since been flushed down the john) toward the bed. That's when I came across Jack Cozine's books, and a dim memory pricked at me. I'd promised to take them to school for him next day.

Anybody as sick as I was should have been in intensive care. I should have had last rites. My heirs should have been planning what to do with their shares. But a promise is a promise, even when made by one drunk to another. So I got dressed--it wasn't easy with my hands shaking like that--and started out to school. Someone, somewhere, was cooking sausage. It took me three tries before I could get past that smell without having to go back and speak to the john.

On the bus, I opened the window. I needed air. Air in Spokane in early April is cold. Some guy behind me objected in purple language, offering to grant me my last wish and and to ensure it was my last unless I closed the window. I turned around and after one look at me he decided he was too late--that anybody that close to death ought to be allowed to open a window.

By the time I got to school, several permanently anchored bits of insides had been shaken loose, and were trying to escape. I managed to get up to our first classroom and leave Jack's books on his desk. I left a note: "Here are your books. I'm going home." No signature, no reason, nothing. Jack and I laughed about that for years.

By evening I was pretty sure I'd live. On the bus ride to Moscow,Idaho I made a game of whether I could make it past the next crossroad without having the driver stop. It was grim. But I won most of the time.

Mother O'Reilly was all solicitation as soon as she saw me. I'm sure she thought her daughter would be a widow before she even got married. When I didn't eat everything in sight--in fact didn't eat anything at all--she became *really* worried. She kept coming around with flu

141

remedies and was so concerned and so nice to me that The O'Reilly couldn't stand it. Finally she said, "MOTHER! He's just hung over."

And that was my condition when I met most of her relatives.

But I started to tell about the apartment, didn't I?

After we were married, we began to notice some disadvantages. For one thing, we'd come home in the evening and the place *stank* Cats. Sometimes the smell hurt your eyes. We soon realized the landlady opened the French doors and came in to use the range in our kitchen, bringing the effluvium of *cat* with her. For twenty-five years I could not bring myself to have a cat around.

When the weather got warmer, we put our bed out on the (enclosed) porch. With the icebox. The first Saturday we slept in, we embarrassed hell out of the iceman when he walked into our "bedroom" with a block of ice. After that, we tried to be up before he got there, but we slept in often enough that we eventually got pretty friendly with him.

Remember the bathroom upstairs? And the roomers? When we'd go up to take a bath, we might have to try a half-dozen times to find the bathroom empty. Then sure as heck, soon as you got in the tub, someone couldn't wait. The best time turned out to be between the time the working people went to bed and the time the taverns closed and the drunks came home.

We only lived there a few months. I went away to work in Twisp that summer (that's another story) and one day The O'Reilly's wallet was stolen and the landlady came home drunk. We knew the time had come to move from our sweet little nest. But it was our first home, and it still has a place in my heart.

First Christmas

When we were married in 1948, we had everything figured out. The O'Reilly planned to keep working (she's a Registered Nurse, remember) until I finished college, then she expected to go back to school. We had this silly idea that the Rhythm Theory worked. It doesn't. The O'Reilly became pregnant immediately. She worked till Thanksgiving, six weeks before the baby was due. We figured that, until she could support us again, we could scrape through on the pittance I got from the G.I. Bill.

Our tiny apartment consisted of a bedroom, living room and a landlady-green kitchen that had once been a closet. We shared a bathroom with another couple. The kitchen's one advantage was its floor; less than four square feet to clean. By the time she quit working, The O'Reilly was barely able to get into the kitchen, and once she was in, she had to back out to turn around.

All the furniture we owned was a bed, so we borrowed furniture from the previous tenants who promised we could use it until spring. They left a tiny refrigerator, a smaller range, a small sofa, a tiny table and two chairs. In the living room we had room for one of two accessories: the ironing board or the playpen; never both.

Semester break came at a convenient time when the Post Office needed extra help during the Christmas rush. For twelve hours a day, nine to nine, seven days a week, I tossed mail sacks. Things were looking up--we had money coming in.

Then the owners of the furniture decided they needed it again. We bought their stove, managed to finance a refrigerator at Wards, and went shopping for other furniture. We walked around Spokane for hours before we found a table and chairs for the princely sum of one hundred four dollars. Thanks to good reports from my home town, we promoted enough credit to get the dining set and a sofa.

All that walking was too much for the baby; he wanted out. So, a week before Christmas, our first child was born. I was up most of that night, then went to my twelve hours of work. When I finally got to the hospital, visiting hours were over and no one was allowed in to see patients. Right then I learned something I've used many times since. All I have to do is act like I belong there and I can wander around any hospital, even on an obstetrics floor. In a Catholic hospital, I steer clear of the nuns, though.

In those days, new mothers stayed in the hospital for at least five days, but The O'Reilly convinced her doctor to send her home after three days so she could prepare for Christmas. We had no tree, there was no money for presents, we'd just gone deeply into worrisome debt, The O'Reilly was so sore she could hardly get around, the poor baby had colic and cried almost constantly, and I was gone for fourteen hours out of the day. Things didn't look good.

But my dear mother-in-law came to help and I had Christmas day off and we were a family. What more does a young couple want for Christmas?

The Down Side

There we were, at the top of this fifteen foot stepladder. I was on the backside, Bill was on the frontside, both of us were giggling hysterically, while the ladder swayed back and forth, back and forth. There was only one way out. I loosened my grip and slid down the legs of the ladder and collapsed, helpless, on the floor. Poor Bill. He slid down his side, too, but he bumped some pretty important parts of his anatomy on every step on the way down. I don't think those bumps had any lasting effect on his sex life, and I know they didn't affect his hysteria. He lay there on the floor beside me, kicking and snorting, and occasionally wiping his eyes.

It was the fall of 1949, and Bill and I were underemployed. Because of some past indiscretions, we found ourselves with wives and kids to support, but without visible means of doing so. We were in college, trying unsuccessfully to live on the 120 bucks a month the Veteran's Administration allowed us. We weren't just poor. Our cash reserves were lower than a nightcrawler's navel, and part-time jobs were about as plentiful as ugly girls in a Diet Pepsi commercial.

Since we didn't have any money, the obvious thing to do was to go into business for ourselves. By borrowing, from our respective sugar bowls, we accumulated enough change to print a few flyers advertising us as "handymen" and "jacks-of-all-trades", we became our own bosses. Hah!! "Own boss" carried about as much truth as our "handy".

We distributed our flyers up on Spokane's South Hill, because that was where all the rich people lived. In our circumstances, we figured anybody who paid at least part of his bills more or less on time *had* to be rich.

We got a job or two as we were handing out the handbills, and we thought we had arrived in fat city. One lady wanted us to take down the screens and put up the storm windows on her house. Seems she was afraid her husband might try it, have a heart attack, and break some of the storm windows.

While we were wrestling with the storm windows, a fellow stopped and watched us in awe. I think he had never seen two guys so obviously lacking in ept, and he probably felt sorry for us. At any rate, Mr. Goodguy (not his real name) asked us if we could change a light fixture for him in his shop downtown. Of course we could, we told him, grovelling side by side at his feet. We'd be only too glad to. We arranged a price--I think it was a whole *five dollars*--and agreed to meet him at his shop at 5 PM on Monday. Spokane closed down at 5 o'clock, and everybody was out of the office buildings and at the bus stops at a few minutes after five.

Mr. Goodguy had a millinery shop on the top floor in one of the old five-story brick buildings that lined Riverside Avenue, Spokane's main street. As we rode up in the elevator, I remarked to Bill that this was exactly like the elevator we'd used when I'd worked for the Display Department of the Sears store in Seattle, back in 1942 and 1943. Those elevators were controlled by a crank, but, at Sears, the Crank wasn't on duty all the time, so we sometimes had to elevate ourselves. The control was a lever that cranked to one side for "UP" and the other side for "DOWN". At Sears, as I told Bill, I'd had to become really good with the elevator, because we had heavy carts to roll in and out, and we had to hit the floor exactly.

Mr. Goodguy wanted us to take down a chandelier from the fifteen-foot (!) ceiling, and put up a flush fixture. Lord knows why. To us, it didn't seem like a big job, and we thought we had a good deal going. He showed us where the stepladder was, paid us, and bade us good night.

Mr. Goodguy was a trusting sort.

The ladder was fifteen feet long, but when it opened up, it was quite a bit short of the ceiling. We reckoned we'd have to work very nearly at the top, and it was sure to be unstable. It would take both of us up on the ladder, too--the chandelier was pretty heavy.

We kept hearing a buzzer ringing, so I wandered out to see what was going on. The elevator was there, door open, and Mr. Goodguy was impatiently pressing the call button. The building superintendent lived in an apartment there on the fifth floor, but he seemed to have gone to bed.

"I'll take you down," I said. "I used to run one of these things in Seattle."

Mr. Goodguy was a trusting sort. Down we went, watching the floors go past--the fourth, the third, the second, to the-- "My gosh," I thought, "it's a long way to the first floor." About the time we passed the third floor, the superintendent's wife came out of her apartment.

"Where's the elevator?"

"Oh, Dick took Mr. Goodguy down. He's run one of these things. Used to work for Sears in Seattle " As Bill babbled along, the Super's wife stood with her arms crossed, tapping her foot.

BLAM !! CRASH !!! TINKLE!!!

"I knew he'd do that," the Super's wife said. Bill, caught in mid-babble, had nothing more to say.

Mr. Goodguy and I weren't hurt. There were big springs at the bottom of the shaft so the shock had been to our psyches, not our bodies. We just looked at each other. I had heard of a "blank expression", but I had never seen one before. I was looking at one now. I was also looking at a blank brick wall where the elevator door should have been. I turned around, and there was the basement floor--about waist high. Some unclean offspring of unmarried parents had moved the first-floor and basement doors to the wrong side of the shaft !!

Mr. Goodguy was cool. He didn't speak or change expression while I helped him up onto the basement floor. He just walked over to the stairway and out into the night.

When Mrs. Super and Bill came clattering down the stairs, I was still standing there in the elevator, wondering what the heck to do now. Mrs. Super took a broom handle and started shoving it at a lot of ancient switches, but the elevator still wouldn't budge.

147

"Oh, well," she said, "My husband will be along in a little while, and he knows how to fix it." She smiled at me, trying to make me feel better. She did. It was nice to start breathing again. Bill reached down a trembling hand and pulled me up to the basement floor. If we'd had a contest for pale right then, he'd probably have won. A bedsheet would have come in third, though.

As we trekked up the stairs, Mrs. Super kept prattling away, but Bill and I, trailing our damaged credibilities behind us, didn't have much to say.

Back to the chandelier. Since I was lighter, I went up the ladder first, then stepped around to the back side. Bill came up, and we went to work on the fixture. One of us--I can't remember which--said, "Hee hee."

That ten-minute job only took us two hours. Every time one of us started up the ladder, one or the other of us giggled, and we rolled on the floor again. Miraculously, though, we finally did manage to get the new fixture installed, and put the ladder away. The elevator was standing there, beckoning seductively with its open door.

"Want to take the elevator down ?" Bill asked.

"No thanks," I said. "I think I'll walk."

I was *not* the trusting sort.

Somebody reported a couple of drunks falling down the stairs, but it was just us, stumbling and giggling and crying and holding onto each other for dear life.

Dempsey's Bar and Grill

My wife and I have been looking for pictures for our living room. When it comes to art, we don't see eye to eye. The O'Reilly goes for the modern, but most modern stuff turns me off. I'm more attracted to the realistic stuff--the more realistic the better. Lately, I've been wishing out loud that I could get a muralist like the one that painted the basement walls of the old Dempsey Hotel in Spokane. His stuff was so realistic it was almost unbelievable, and I used to admire it and discuss it at length with Dempsey's night bartender, whose name, no kidding, was Art.

In my senior year in college, I worked full time for what was then the top juke box operation in Spokane. Our equipment was not actually juke boxes, though. We had a studio wired to individual speaker/microphone units in the taverns and restaurants. When the customer dropped in a nickel (shows you how long ago *that* was) a sexy female voice asked him to name a selection from a menu on the unit. The menu showed three hundred or so selections--better than the newest and best jukebox, the "Hundred Record Seeberg". The sexy voice was a real attraction to the skid row winos. I suspect those operators offered the only pleasant words some of those guys ever got. What the drunks didn't know was that, though some of the owners of those sexy voices were as pretty as promised, others were fugitives from the dog pound.

My job was supposedly maintenance, but I also collected all those nickels and split them with the house, did installations, handled the complaints of the customers and the bartenders, and soothed the ruffled feathers of the operators, as well as defending the studio from the occasional amorous drunk who had fallen head-over-heels (easy for *him* to do) in love with the voice from the jukebox.

The studio was in the old four-story Dempsey Hotel, in what used to be Spokane's skid row. Dempsey's and all the places like it are gone now--victims of the 1974 World's Fair--but at that time, the Hotel was just beginning to overcome its reputation as a former house of ill-repute. The upper floors were accessible by a stairway that opened right on the street, rather than through what had been the lobby, and occasionally an old customer of the former tenants tried to come up to see the "girls." Our studio occupied the second floor, but the third and fourth floors were vacant, except for an occasional wino who found his way in and went to sleep on the floor. Once in a while, when one would wake up in the throes of the D. T.'s and thump around overhead, the girls would be in a panic until I got there to throw the poor, harmless devil out.

The first floor had been converted into a single room bar, pool hall, card room, cafeteria, and restaurant. It was so big, you couldn't see one end from the other through the smoke. The whole place stank of old beer and vomit and cheap cigars, and the floors were sprinkled with sawdust and passed out winos. Altogether, it was a really high class place.

John Dempsey (no relation to the former heavyweight champion) ran the saloon. John and his night bartender, Art, were a pair--each about six foot four or five and maybe 270 pounds. They were the closest of friends, like "pardners" in the Old West. They were rough and tough, yet still tolerant and gentle and generous like most skid row bartenders, and were my very good friends. When you work skid row weighing 126 pounds and look too young to drink, you make sure you are on good terms with guys like that.

Back in the Dempsey Hotel's better days, before the reform, when the upstairs had been a whorehouse, the card room had been a high-class poker parlor, but in my time, only the basement still held the aura of opulence that had once been part of the place.

Ah, that basement!! Few people, except for Dempsey's employees, got to see the basement in those days. I was one of the lucky few because, for one, I had to poke around our music system cables. Another entry

150

came along with my friendship with Art. After we had both worked late, we sometimes had a few drinks in the privacy of the basement. He was the one who showed me around the beautifully done murals which still graced the walls. The artist's name was unfamiliar to me at the time, but I have since come to know that he was one of the top Western painters, and ranked up near Remington as a recorder of the Old West. He was good!! Many of the paintings looked so real I imagined I could walk right into them.

Hidden away in one of the rooms which were then used for storage was the best, the most realistic, painting I've ever seen. In the foreground, a mountain lion crouched on a rock, so real that I could have sworn his tail twitched. In the background, a herd of deer browsed on the hill, the big buck watching a nearby spike buck. Art and I used to pass through that room when we'd stay late. First time, I shied around the lion, and Art ribbed me about it.

"Real, ain't it?" he'd said. "Bet you could walk right into that picture." The way he said it gave me the shivers. It was too true. "Lookit that old panther watchin' them deer. Reckon he's thinkin' they'd make good eatin'. Can't say I blame him. Say, speakin' of eatin', ever eat that stew upstairs?"

I had. It went for thirty-five cents a bowl, and was often all the winos ate all winter. I looked closely at the deer herd, and there was something in Art's joking that made them seem even more than real. Come to think of it, the stew did sometimes taste like venison.

I was fascinated by that picture. Whenever Art left me alone down there, I'd go in and stare at it and imagine myself in it and I'd count the deer in the herd. At first I thought there were thirteen, then a few weeks later I could only count twelve. If I'd had a drink or two, the lion's tail indeed seemed to twitch, and I could almost see the old buck shaking his rack at the spike. Then the cold chills would hit me again and I'd have to get out of there.

Late one night in mid-winter, Art and I closed up late. Neither of us was in a hurry to go out in the cold without some antifreeze, so we went downstairs to the old bar. We had talked for an hour or so, and I had ignored what seemed like hints that I might want to leave, when Art went behind the bar and took a rifle off the rack of guns that stood there.

"Boss wants some stew meat," he said. "Make yourself at home with the bottle, and let yourself out when you want to go home."

I got up to leave, but Art motioned me back.

"Don't leave on account of me. Place is yours for a while. Just lock up when you leave." He left by way of the room with my favorite picture. I reckoned he was going to jacklight a deer out where the mountains came down into the outskirts of Spokane, but what the heck. I wasn't the game warden.

I did what Art had said to do. I made myself so at home that I went to sleep (or passed out, I'm not sure which) and only woke up when Art came back in. He was carrying a little spike buck, freshly killed and dressed out, over one shoulder, with the rifle slung over the other.

"You still here?" He seemed really startled to see me. "Look," he said, "don't say anything to anybody about this, will ya?" He nodded toward the buck that he'd dumped on the floor. I shook my head. Hell, it wasn't any of my business how Dempsey fed half the winos in Spokane so cheap. I saw by the clock above the bar that it was nearly morning, and I had a class at eight o'clock.

On my way out, I looked over at that splendidly realistic mural. The cat still sat on the rock, and, out of habit, I counted the deer. Eleven? The old boss buck seemed to be looking at me, rather than watching the spike buck as usual. I rubbed my eyes, but it didn't do any good--there just wasn't any spike buck there.

I never got down into that part of the basement after that. Art and I both got really busy for a while, and we didn't seem to be able to get together. Then Art just disappeared. I asked around but nobody seemed to know where he'd gone. It was right at that time that John Dempsey was hauled off to the nuthouse in Medical Lake, so I couldn't ask him.

John's was a weird case. Seems he'd been fine up to the time he broke down. He'd hired a painter to come in at night and repaint some of the stairwells, but the painter had gone too far and painted over some of he murals. When the morning crew came in, they found John down there, crying and babbling something about "He's in there!" as he scrubbed at the wall where the mountain lion had been. When they tried to stop him, John had gone on a rampage and chased them all out. It took a dozen cops to haul John away.

With both Art and John gone, and even after John came back from "the Lake", Dempsey's just wasn't the same. It wasn't as friendly, and the price of stew went way up, so I hardly ever went in there--only on company business, as a matter of fact. I saw John a few times, but he was so changed that talking to him made me feel funny, and I didn't like to ask him about Art. After I quit the wired music business I lost touch with him, too.

Art and John must be getting pretty old now. I wonder where they are.

For Prunella

Just for you I make this rhyme:

I think of you all the time.

Sure, your knees knock when you walk,

Sure, your teeth click when you talk.

Sure, your nose is red and shiny,

Sure, your voice is kind of whiney.

You'll inherit that gold mine.

Won't you be my Valentine?

Bear Story

Everybody who's done much tent camping or backpacking has at least one bear story to tell. Many true stories are downright terrifying, especially if they are about grizzlies. Many of them were frightening at the time, but turn out to be hilarious later on. The bear gets bigger with every telling, and the results get funnier. My bear story is *not* about a big bear--this one was only half grown or so, and he didn't seem really frightening at all. Except that he *was* a bear, and even half-grown black bears are nothing to fool with, I found out.

In the summer of 1967, I had accrued four weeks' vacation. By judicious scheduling so as to include the July 4th holiday I was able to stretch it to a full 30 days. So The O'Reilly and I took two cars, two tents, ten children, leave of our senses, a big pile of sleeping bags and blankets, camp stove, snakebite kit, plenty of aspirin, and set out on a camping trip that took us through half a dozen states, including visits to both sets of grandparents and various friends and relatives.

At the time, our four older boys were 18, 17, 16, and 15, and our next younger boy was 11. Our girls were 6, 8, and 13 years old, and our two youngest boys were 2 and 4. We divided the sleeping space so the five older boys had the privacy of one tent, and the rest of us--all the girls, the two youngest boys, and mom and dad--slept in the other. This agreed with the sleeping arrangements we had at home, and the kids referred to the the "upstairs" tent where the older boys were, and the "downstairs" tent where the rest of us slept.

We camped at a number of places along the way-- in the mosquitoes and redwoods of California, in the mosquitoes and snow at Crater Lake, Oregon, and in the mosquitoes and cold in Idaho. As we went farther north, it became more difficult to get our smaller children, accustomed to Southern California, to bed and asleep at night. In the northern latitudes the sun sometimes stays around until 9:30 or 10 at night and dusk lasts until 11 or so. When we intended to get up in the morning and make an early start, we preferred to have the little ones in bed early. It's very difficult, however, to convince a 2-year-old or a 4-year-old to go to sleep while the sun's still shining. It's even more difficult to convince a 16- or 17-year-old.

In the downstairs tent, in order to make the little boys sleepy, Daddy began telling stories. We lay there in our sleeping bags while I told any story that happened to come into my head. My stories concerned the animals that might live in the areas where we camped, and were generally sympathetic toward the animals and their troubles. I avoided allowing them contact with men--no sex or violence in *my* stories.

One night I told about Elmo Elk and all his troubles with wolves, snow, starvation conditions in the winter, and how he finally broke through the fence to the farmer's hay. Another night I told about a squirrel, and later about a chipmunk--animals we had seen during the day.

156

The Clearwater Forest is at a latitude and in a time zone where the sun doesn't go down until very late. We had camped there one night and day, and we went to bed early the second night, intending to start early the next morning. The sun was still high, and the children very cross, with no intention of going to sleep.

I began the story of Bucky Beaver. I told of Bucky's childhood and of the construction of the Beaver House where he was raised. I told how he learned to cut trees, and how he had learned to help build a dam. Then I stopped. From the far corner of the tent came a small voice: "Go on, Daddy."

So I continued, telling about the time of the flood when a hole appeared in the dam and it seemed as if the whole dam would go; and how Bucky Beaver bravely cut a tree, plugged the hole and became a hero. After this I stopped again. Then, from my 13-year-old-daughter: "Well go on, Daddy."

Bucky Beaver continued. I took him through various adventures, eventually marrying him off and sending him to go and build his own dam. Finally, when I stopped talking, there was no response. Everyone was asleep.

By this time, the sun had gone down and darkness had settled. I lay there wondering, *If I have to do this every night, what am I going to tell about tomorrow night?*

The night was very still when I heard a small sound from outside. We're experienced campers and always put the food in the car. This night, most of the food was in the car, although some was in the upstairs tent with the insatiable teenage appetites, and I wasn't concerned about animals in the camp. But, when the sounds outside continued, I got up to see what was going on. I looked around and saw, nuzzling at the entrance of the boys' tent, a *small bear*. Well, I didn't think *that* was such a good idea. Perhaps I should get rid of him. The only thing handy to throw was an extra tent pole, pointed on one end. I threw it like a javelin, and my aim was never better; the pole scored a perfect goose. The bear let a out a sound of *Maaaaw,* lunged forward, and found himself inside the tent, standing on several teenage boys who began shouting uncouth and uncomplimentary things at him. They were well protected in their sleeping bags, and the bear wasn't interested in eating boys. He just wanted to get the heck out of there, but he couldn't find his way.

Dad came to the rescue, wearing nothing but shorts. I seized the deadliest weapon we had--a hatchet--and dashed toward the boys' tent. I threw open the fly (of the *tent,* Mabel). Out came the bear--between my legs. Suddenly, I was riding the bear bareback and backward, waving a hatchet and shouting unprintable words.

My bearback ride in the Clearwater Forest didn't last for more than a few seconds. The bear shot under a tree limb and I was knocked to the ground. Except for our dignities, neither the bear nor I was hurt. As I lay there under the tree, feebly waving the hatchet and thinking about what a picture it must have been between the time the bear emerged from the tent and time he passed the tree, I began to laugh. It must have been better than a Laurel and Hardy skit. The more I thought about it, the more I laughed.

The O'Reilly poked me in the ribs, and said, "What on earth are you laughing at?"

I was laughing so hard I couldn't tell her, so I turned over and went back to sleep.

Saturday Night at the Hoskins House

Members of my family relate events of the year 1969 with reference to a series of catastrophes. Put together some fifty-two nights like the one described here, and you will have an idea why.

At the time, Mommy was over 21, Pop was overweight, Mike was twenty, Jim nineteen, John Kerry seventeen, Kevin sixteen, Steve twelve, Brian six, and Tim four. The girls were fourteen (Chris), ten (Theresa), and eight (Jean).

Of course, it never rains in Southern California but the sun had been shining heavily for a week. Not just briefly, but in sheets. The gutters ran full of sunshine, and the back yard was a quagmire. Cars stalled in intersections. Have you ever had sunshine in your distributor? It got so bad that, no matter where you wanted to go, you just couldn't get there from here.

Cabin fever was epidemic. Brian and Tim, normally free to roam barefoot about the neighborhood, considered this particular weather a personal affront, and took their frustrations at enforced confinement out on each other, their mother, and especially, their sisters, invading the girls' room and indiscriminately scattering their treasures. The girls reacted, as girls will, with screams and tears and tattling until poor Mommy, fighting the flu and sick of it all was ready to climb the walls.

Then came Saturday night. The house was overflowing with Hoskinses. Everyone was really uptight, and since late afternoon, the walls had been shaking and the timbers rattling with the calls of sub-adult homo-sapiens ("Shut *up!*") and the adult ("Go to your *room!*").

Mike and Jim, cowards that they were, took refuge with their friend, Jim Farris, who was home from the seminary recovering from some dreadful (and highly contagious) disease. Brian had started so many fights and been sent to his room so many times he had finally

159

gone to sleep, and refused to get up, even for supper. Kerry decided he, too, wanted to get out.

"Where are you going?"

"Oh, you know Mom. Probably Hollywood."

"Come on. Where ARE you going?"

"Oh, Mom, course I'm gonna go out and get drunk and smoke some Pot and try some LSD and everything like that." So we knew he was going to a Youth For Christ rally. No matter how carefully you train them, they will still do things like that.

Kevin had been on the phone off and on all afternoon. (Or off and on the phone all afternoon.) At about nine o'clock he announced that he needed a car to go to a a party. And he'd promised to pick up Larry.

"Where's the party?"

"You know that tract just across Brookhurst? It's in there."

"Where does Larry live?"

"Right down by church. Don't worry, Dad. There aren't any bad intersections I have to go through."

"All right, but take the F-85. It's the best rain car. But it's clear out of gas. Stop at the service station right down on the corner; don't try to go any farther or you won't make it. And remember to hit the puddles real slow."

"OK, Dad, but gimme some money."

Next to "What's for supper?" this was the most frequent sentence in the Hoskins house: "Gimme some money."

At about nine thirty the telephone rang and The O'Reilly answered.

"Yes, Kevin. *What?* It's *what?*" Then to Pop. "It's Kevin. He ran out of gas and said something about the car being wrecked, but not bad. He wants to talk to you." So Pop got on the phone.

"What's the matter, Kev?"

"I ran out of gas right at Larry's, and we pushed the car down here and can't get it started."

"Where are you?"

"At the service station right across from the church. The gas runs all over the engine and they guy here says if it does start, it'll catch fire. He says some gasket is all wrecked up."

"Oh. You're flooded. how old is this guy?"

"Oh, about 20, I guess."

"Yeah. He don't know beans. But I'd better come down. Be there in a minute." So poor Pop hunted up car-fixing clothes and drove down to the station. With the air filter off, sure enough, throttle full down, gas spurted all over the engine. The expert mechanic was turning off all the lights 'cause he was going home, so it was pretty hard to see, but at least he was staying to heck out of the way. After Pop gave couple of good hard taps on the float to loosen it, the engine started right up. And, incidentally, the cupful or so of gas on the block did *not* catch fire.

"OK, Kevin. Now, if it gives you any more trouble, you can start it by floor-boarding it. If it does act up, I want to know. Tomorrow."

Pop was home again by 10:30, soaking wet, and, as soon as he cleaned up a bit, in bed. We had just turned off the television, when we heard a strange scuffling noise in the hall. Our bedroom door opened. It was Kerry.

"Hey, Dad. I think I broke my foot."

"What?"

"I hurt my foot real bad, and I think I broke it." So Pop got up again and started out into the hall--in his shorts. "Dad, you better get dressed. There might be someone here."

"Who?" Picturing the police, or something.

"Al and Mary and Helen brought me home."

"Did they help you in?"

"No. I just hopped in." By this time, Pop had his pants on and Kerry was sprawled on a chair in the living room. Al and company were gone.

"How did you do it?" we asked, as we took off his shoe as carefully as possible.

"I jumped off a car."

161

"Jumped off a car? How come?" Kerry read my mind.

"Aw, it wasn't moving, Dad. I was up on it giving a speech like this guy we heard tonight--*ow*. Dammit, that *hurts*."

"Where?"

"Here under my little toe, and in the ball behind my big toe, and back here in my ankle."

"OK. Lie down and we'll elevate it." So he lay down on the living room couch, hanging over at both ends. It was only a six-foot couch, so we brought a chair to hold the leftover.

"Dick, shall we get the G.P. from the clinic or an orthopedic specialist?" The O'Reilly asked.

"Well, the G.P. is in tonight. Maybe he could look at it and then have Dr. Lee look at it Monday."

"Well, you realize if he looks at it and finds it broken he'll put a cast on it and we'll be stuck with it. We can't go to Dr. Lee then."

"Please, Dad, let's do *something*. It hurts like hell."

"Here, take these," and we gave him two aspirin and a POI[1] pill.

We decided on Dr. Lee, who had treated Pop's sprained ankle, and whom we liked very much. His answering service couldn't find him but promised to call back in a few minutes. We waited. And waited.

At twelve-fifteen, Mike came home. Kerry was almost asleep with his foot elevated on a big stack of worn-out pillows which we had, fortunately, forgotten to throw away that morning. Poor old Pop was sound asleep in the recliner chair.

Pop woke up when Mike said, "What happened to you?"

So Kerry explained again. "I jumped off a car and broke my foot."

---

[1] POI-- very strong tranquilizer. Makes you feel like "P-on-it".

"Oh, good grief. I cawn't stand it. I simply cawn't stand it," said Mike in his best English accent, pacing about with his typically dramatic palm-to-forehead gesture.

"Where's Jim? Didn't you bring him home with you?" Pop asked.

"Jim will be home when the bar closes." I must explain that Jim Farris' parents owned a bar, and, when they closed at 2 AM they frequently returned any Hoskins' they found lying about. In their house, not in the bar.

"I don't think we'll find Dr. Lee, if they haven't found him yet," The O'Reilly said. "Sometimes these doctors just won't be bothered at night. Believe me, I have a lot of experience with them from the hospital."

"Let's try him again anyway." So we called the answering service and found they had no record of a call to Dr. Lee. We had called before just as the shift changed at the answering service, and the message got lost. The girl had Dr. Lee on the phone in three minutes.

"How far are you from the hospital?" he wanted to know.

"Fifteen minutes, at most."

"OK. I'll meet your there in half an hour. I'll call them to be expecting you." So Kerry hopped out to the car--he wouldn't let anyone help him--and off we went through the puddles of sunshine to the hospital. We could almost drive this route in our sleep, by then, because our clinic was just across the street, and there had been Steve's broken arm, and then there was Timmy and there was The O'Reilly's operation and Kerry's broken shoulder and the time he stepped on a basketball (that's what I said--stepped on a basketball) and Pop's operation besides various other little odds and ends of emergencies.

The X-Ray technician was waiting with a wheelchair. They weren't very busy, fortunately. People were staying home off the lousy streets instead of smashing themselves up on the freeways. One middle-aged couple was standing around trying to get some information, and no one was about to give them any. I gathered that the person they are interested in was asleep in the car and they wanted to know whether he (or she) should go to a sanitarium or not.

While the X-Ray technician took pictures, the orderly wanted to fill out the form but he'd only started when a young man came rushing in with a 3-year-old who was really gasping for breath. He thought the kid had swallowed something, so the orderly left to see about him while Pop fills out the form. We'd never had a kid with croup,[2] but the orderly was familiar with it and in three minutes had the kid breathing comfortably again. Meanwhile, Pop was working on the Form.

Form: Was this an accident?

I was tempted to write, "No. He broke his foot on purpose."

Pop: Yes.

Form: If answer is yes, how did it happen?

Pop: He jumped off a car and hurt his foot.

Presently, Kerry came back from X-Ray, the orderly had the croupy kid comfortable, the form was on the desk, and Pop was in the back room talking to Kerry. Now here came the orderly with the form in his hand.

"How did it happen?"

"He jumped off a car."

"A moving car?"

"No, it was standing still." By this time Kerry looked like he'd like to forget the whole thing. Hardened as he was, the Orderly padded away mumbling and shaking his head.

Dr. Lee came breezing in. He's oriental, six feet, and must have weighed two hundred pounds, all muscle. You just looked at him and liked him. You'd *better* when he's that size. He was very professional. He read the report without batting an eye. (In my sleepy state, I

---

2 At the time this happened, we'd never had croup at our house. Within the next week, Timmy came in with croup so bad he was nearly scared to death. Fortunately, The O'Reilly knew just what to do.

wondered: do orientals "bat" their eyes. Perhaps they "bird" them or "bee" them. Oh, Hell.)

Dr. Lee's questions were pointed. "How high did you jump from?"

"Just off the hood."

"Did you twist your foot or feel anything pop?"

"No, I don't think so."

Dr. Lee's competent fingers found every sore place on the foot in no time at all. It was easy to tell, because Kerry was swearing through gritted teeth, and in a cold sweat. Dr. Lee suddenly walked out. He was gone maybe three minutes, and came back with:

"Well, you don't have any broken bones. You have a badly sprained ankle."

"But doctor. It hurts down here under my toes." The doctor shrugged.

"Pulled tendons. I'll tape it up, and you must try to stay off it for a day or two."

While he wrapped it, Pop asked, "Should I get him some crutches?"

"No, not unless he really needs them If he's careful and stays off cars," Dr. Lee was grinning impishly now, "he should be able to get along without them. And I'll want to see him in my office in a few days. Make an appointment for him for--let's see--Friday."

"I need an excuse to get out of P.E., Dad"

"Sure thing," and Dr. Lee handed Kerry a prescription blank which said, "No P.E. for 2-3 weeks." And Dr. Lee was gone like a genie.

As we left, we saw the couple that wanted information talking to a policeman, so we still have a great curiosity. Was it a teen-age child they found on drugs? Was it a parent who was senile and inclined to run away? (The O'Reilly had ninety-six of them in the hospital where she worked. Senile patients, not parents.) Were they complaining to the cop about the treatment given them? We'll never know.

With Kerry hopping on one foot, we arrived home. By the time he hopped upstairs, and Pop's adrenaline was down to a tolerable level and he'd gone to bed, it was close to 3 AM.

Four o'clock. Our bedroom door opened.

"Mommy," said Brian, "I can't sleep;" Of course he couldn't. He'd slept for eleven hours already, and he'd missed his supper, remember? Guess we should get up and feed him, but he said, "Can I have a radio?"

"Is that all you need, Brian?"

"Yes," with a long sigh. "If I have a radio, I won't be lonesome." After only twenty minutes or so, we managed to find a transistor radio with a live battery, and Brian was back in bed.

Five o'clock. Our bedroom door opened as quietly as if by a breeze. Instantly, Pop was half awake. This time it was Timmy, carrying a blanket and pillow. Apparently Brian's radio woke him up.

"I 'cared, Daddy"

"Do you want to come in bed with me?"

"No-o-o."

"Do you want to sleep on the rug?"

"Uh-huh." He curled up on the floor with his blanket and pillow and was asleep. Pop was half.

Five forty-five. The alarm blares. On *Sunday*. For Christmas, Kevin and Steve bought their Dad a beautiful calendar alarm clock. Couldn't take it to work--afraid it might be stolen. It had one quirk. Whenever it was wound, the alarm button popped out. Somebody wound it Saturday. Pop stumbled over shoes and poor Timmy and finally found the cockeyed thing and turned it off.

After a while, Pop dozed off again, and dreamed of jumping off cars into puddles of muddy sunshine filled with croupy kids that are lonesome and need a radio to keep them company. Pretty soon, he got up and made coffee. Why not? It's Fathers Day.

The Argument

Brian starts the argument again as soon as we're settled in the car.

"Aw, Pop. You don't understand. Jeannine'll think I'm a dork. She knows I got my license and if I don't show up with a car, she'll think I'm a bay-bee." His friends sit silent, but I know they side with him.

"I told you, no. Not 'til you've had more experience. You only got your license last month." On his sixteenth birthday, as a matter of fact, and now he thinks he's Andy Granatelli.

"But I've been driving since Christmas. You said yourself I'm a good driver."

"You are, but you've never driven at night."

"I never will if you have your way." His voice is sullen.

I glance in the rear-view mirror. The wind from the open window is playing with his hair. He tosses his head back to get the hair out of his eyes, but it doesn't help. The sun-bleached hair is so long and fine that it clings to his face. He lifts the strand between his fingers and draws it back, putting it in its exact place. Even though he's furious, that hair has to be just right.

"Now, Brian," I say, still trying to reason with him. "You'll have to go out at night with me or your mother first."

"Sure." Then he mocks me. "Drive with me or muh-ther." It's an angry chant.

"Brian!" He's getting to me, and he knows it.

"You never *let* me drive. Like now. You tell me to get experience, then you won't let me drive. It isn't *fair*. Geez." He flops around in the seat, his signal of disgust.

I glance in the mirror again. He's glaring at me, but when he sees me looking, he turns away. But not so soon I miss the sadness in his face. Poor kid! It's hell to be sixteen.

I pull onto the beach parking lot and park. The boys spill out, arguing about their boogie boards, in a hurry to get to the water. Except Brian. He gets out last, deliberately, making a point of not looking at me, then swaggers away carrying his board and fins, his muscles a washboard that scrubs the inside of his tan. He's so tall! Last year he barely came to my shoulder; this year I barely come to his. I watch him stride across the sand, tossing his head every few steps to flip his hair back, then he's gone behind a dune.

I gather up my towel and suntan oil and shirt and radio and slog through the deep sand toward the water. Halfway across the beach I have to drop my towel and dance on it to keep from blistering my feet. Those kids, barefoot year-round, think nothing of a little scorching sand. *They* blister their feet when they wear shoes.

The boys are already out beyond the sandbar, where the waves break first and highest. They look so near as I stand on the dune above the water line, but I know that, from out there, the shore seems a long way away. I used to go out there too, but this year I'll stay close inshore. I'm really out of shape. And heavy. "Pudgy Pop," Brian calls me when he thinks he can get away with it. I bathe myself in suntan oil, and stretch out on my towel to just relax.

I never know if I sleep at the beach. The warmth of the sun, the smell of seaweed, the splash of breakers, the screams of the children, indistinguishable from the seagulls, all might as well be dream as reality. When I rouse, the towel is soaked with sweat and suntan oil, and it clings to my body when I sit up. I look for the boys, and see them still out with the big waves, clustered together, seeking the best surf. One white board lies alone out past the break. That will be Brian, sulking and feeling sorry for himself.

I walk down to the wet sand and let a dying breaker wash around my feet. The water's icy! A few more steps and another wave pours around my knees. This one isn't quite so cold. Only one thing to do--walk straight at the in-rolling waves, and meet the next one with my chest. The chilly water pushes hard. My feet curl into the sand to keep from sliding backward. I dive to meet the next swell, surface, dive into the next.

The water's warmer now. Waist-deep in the trough between the waves, I stand waiting for a decent breaker. Around me, others, strangers, also wait, examining each wave like judges in a contest, testing some, diving through those that break wrong. Occasionally, one chooses a wave, rising with it and disappearing in a surge of foam. My wave comes, and I swim with it, try to reach the crest as it breaks, but fall behind instead as it races toward the beach. Again I wait, again I try, again I fail. Then comes the perfect break, and I ride like a chip on the rushing comber, glorying in the speed and one with the foam until the wave and I are spent on the sand.

It only takes a few waves to tire me out. After my fourth (or is it fifth?) ride, my arms are tired and I'm puffing, but still I stagger out to try just once more. An ebbing wave tugs at me and my weakened legs give way. I float with the ebb and ride over the next breaker. In the trough I try to stand but I can't reach bottom. I swim a few strokes toward the shore and see the other body-surfers two wave-crests away. Why so far? And they're moving! No, I am! I'm in the rip! I'm being carried out! I try to scream for help, but a crossing wave crashes, unexpected, over me. I struggle free, choking, not swimming now, only clawing at the water. The buoyancy of mind and body are gone, and panic drags at my senses and limbs. My heart beats against its cage like a madman.

A shred of sanity tells me, *float!* I have to float; the rip will run out under me. I turn onto my back, arch my body. Another swell sloshes over my face. Again I choke and retch. I swim my upper body free, and, an eternity later, gather in a decent breath. The effort costs. My weighted arms respond slowly, my legs ache from the unaccustomed strain. I fall back, face down, and forcibly calm my breath, resisting the racking strain when my body wants to cough. The discipline cools my panic. I take one breast stroke, one gasp of air. The shore's so

169

far--it seems like half a mile. I'll never make it that far. I'd scream, but who could hear me? I can barely hear the boom of the surf. The gentle splash of waves sounds like voices chiding me for my foolishness.

"Hey! You okay?" A real voice! I turn toward it, try to call for help, but only choke. I see a flash of white, a blurred head.

"Jesus Christ! Pop! Here!" It's Brian. I try to call his name. It comes out a sob. A rubber-like surface strikes my shoulder. Without volition, my hands scrabble for a grip, touch flesh, seize like a predator on prey.

"No! Stop that!" There's fear and anger in Brian's voice. A stunning force strikes my arm. My hand tears free. "The board," he says. "Hold the board." My hands finally obey. Brian's voice is calm, now. "You're all right, Pop. It's *okay*." It's a command. "Rest on the board a minute. You're okay," he repeats.

Lying half-on the board, I weep my panic away. My fingers relax their deadly grip, and I begin to breathe the rhythm of the waves. Finally Brian says, "Let's go in now. Here's the tether." I feel him tie it to my wrist. "If you spill, let go the board. The tether'll keep it with you. Okay?"

I try to ask, "What about you?" but it comes out nothing. Brian seems to understand.

"I've got fins," he says. "I'll be right along. Hold the front of the board, bend it up, let it carry you. Just like body surfing, only easier. Here's a wave. Go!" I feel a surge as he pushes the board. A sea breaks under me and I'm flying upward, then plunging forward in a crazy rollercoaster ride toward the shore. The wave peters out, and I turn to look for Brian. I see him cresting a breaker, tumbling with it, disappearing, reappearing in the foam. The wave rolls in and shoots me shoreward. I give myself to board and waves and let them take me in. At last I reach the inshore breaker, rise on it above the body surfers.

I'm too far up. The wave meets the ebb and topples forward, discards me like a useless plaything, then grinds me into the hard-packed sand. I lie there stunned while the ebb buries my limbs in bits of broken shell, and the boogie board pulls at the tether like an impatient puppy. Then Brian's beside me, his hand gentle on my shoulder.

"All right, Pop?"

I nod, not daring to answer yet.

Brian pulls the tether from my wrist and gathers up the board. I get up slowly, feel his hand ready on my arm, stumble up the beach out of reach of the water, then drop to the sand again, lying flat, exhausted. Brian slumps down nearby, and sits staring at the waves, letting sand pour through his fingers. After a time, I try to speak, but can only clear my throat. Brian looks at me, then turns and carefully examines the angry scratches on his arm. Finally, he grins at me--the first time all day.

"Y'know, I think I'll sue," he says. It feels good to laugh. Brian stands up and brushes off the sand. "Time to go home," he says. "I'll get the others." I watch him stride out into the waves and plunge toward the sandbar and the outer breakers.

All right, Jeannine Who-ever-you-are. Be impressed tonight. It will be the first time he's driven after dark.

Learning
1969

Once you were three.
You came to my workshop, blond and cherubic
And watched with wond'ring eyes.
Your baby voice lisped, Can I help too?
And I said, Don't come in here.
The tools are too sharp, and you'll be in the way.
The smile left your eyes, and tears took its place.
I didn't know what else to say, so I turned back to my
    work.
And you toddled away.

Once you were six.
You came to my chair, proud of the worthless prize you
    had won.
In your little boy's voice, you said
Daddy, look what I've got.
Why don't you come to Sunday school with Mommy and
    me?
And I said, Daddy's tired.
Just go change your clothes.
I reached for my beer and watched the Rams line up on
    TV.
You tore your prize in two, and dropped it in the trash.
And you skipped away.

Once you were seven.
You took candy from a store and didn't pay.
I made you take it back and tell the manager,
And, angry and embarrassed, I drove home fast.
I got a ticket and I bawled the cop out as you cringed in
    back.
And when we got home, you said you were sorry
But I laughed and said, Don't worry
I know the judge and will get it fixed tomorrow.

Then I told you never to take anything without paying for
    it again.
You looked at me a long, long time.
Then you walked away.

Once you were nine.
Breathless, you came to me with the news.
Dad, I've got a new friend. Boy, can he play ball.
I said, Who is he? Where is he from?
And you said, Well, Dad. He's not like us.
He's poor and he's black. But he sure can play ball.
And I said, Try to understand
I'm not prejudiced, you see, but what will the neighbors
    think?
And you turned and ran away.

Once you were twelve.
You came to my room on Saturday morn
And asked, Dad, is marijuana so bad?
So many say yes and so many say no.
I know kids who use it and think it has less kick than
    beer.
What's the truth, Dad?
And I answered, Get out of my room.
My head aches, I'm sick. I forget what I did
Last night and I'm worried I tee'd off my boss.
Just stay off the drugs, or you'll catch it from me.
And you slipped away.

Once you were eighteen.
You said to me, Dad, why the hate and the fear?
Why the war in a country I never heard of?
I answered you gruffly, You silly young punk
When you've been where I have and seen what I have
What the other side wants--
Their system, not ours, where the hypocrite reigns.
Get drafted. Go learn about Life in the War.
You looked at me strangely.
Then you drove away.

173

Once you were twenty.
I went to your campus, appalled by the turmoil and
 strikes.
I went to see you and I wasn't prepared.
You were bearded and long-haired, and dressed so I
 hardly knew you.
Your room smelled of incense and bodies and Grass.
And I said to you, What has become
Of the things I have taught you?
Of honesty, reverence, honor, respect?
Have you learned none of them now?
And you said to me, Go away, Old Man.
I'm learning.

Today I looked at you for the last time.
A Guardsman, policeman--no one knows who--
Pulled a trigger--in my name--
And now you lie still.
You're going away.
There's one thing you should know.
I'm learning.

Boss Cat

I have my paraphernalia--chair, notebook, pencils, and a tape recorder with some classical music--in the sunny back yard. I intend to catch some rays while I do a little writing. For some reason, I look toward the tool shed in the corner of the yard. Is that a yellow shirt someone has tossed away? No, it's a cat. Boy, look at the size of that head and neck. Got to be an unaltered tom, and probably boss of the neighborhood. At least, if I were a cat, he'd have *my* vote.

He looks like he's dead, sprawled in the shade of my backyard wall. Was he there when I sat down? Or did he just come along and decide to be sociable? I speak to him, to see if my voice would startle him.

"Hello, cat."

Not even a whisker moves.

"Hey, cat. You OK?"

Still no movement except the rise and fall of his chest as he pants out the heat.

I'm sitting here looking at him, admiring his ability to relax so completely. He lies there touching as much ground with as much of his body as he can. Suddenly, he starts. His head comes up and he glares at me, his muscles ready to take him away in a flash. Has my staring frightened him? Oh, there's my own cat, stroking her tail along my leg. She came up silently, and I'm sure the yellow cat couldn't have heard her over the noise of the tape recorder.

What sense told him of the newcomer? Surely not one of the five we humans boast. He identified her at 20 yards or so as an unknown. He's not afraid of me, though he's a bit standoffish, and he certainly can't be afraid of my cat. But some ancient instinct told him, *"Unknown!"* and he reacted by going instantly from complete relaxation to full alert. Without a lot of emotion and adrenaline. How I envy him.

When I look up after writing this, he's gone. Involuntarily, I say, "Hey, where'd he go?" He raises his massive head in the garden and looks at me, not in alarm but as if to answer my question. His huge yellow eyes look me over in reproach, then he sinks back and relaxes.

My cat decides to look into this stranger, and she strolls stiff-legged toward him. The big tom raises his head and watches her. She pretends to ignore him, and laying her ears back, walks past him behind a row of beans, then stalks along until only the row of beans is between them.

The tom gets up slowly, and, ears forward and neck stretched fully, leans toward her. She lets him get within an inch, then she spits explosively, and his neck contracts like a released spring, his ears fall back, and his expression is one of confusion and annoyance. I stifle a guffaw. How I feel for him! What male among us has not had that experience? A female shows interest, but when the interest is reciprocated, the response is one of anger. Who knows the female mind? Of course, he may have made an indelicate suggestion, for all I know.

The tom strolls away, along the row of beans. At the end of the row, she intercepts him again. All is forgiven. They touch noses a few times, the way we humans make small talk. But she's not in heat--never will be, as a matter of fact--so he turns and, looking bored, ambles to the corner of the yard, where, with a single effortless spring, he reaches to top of the fence. He walks along the fence to the neighbors' shrubbery, looks back at me once, then disappears, and I see him no more.

Some are Mice, Some are not so Mice

One day a few years ago I found evidence that a mouse had taken up housekeeping in our garage. When I announced the discovery, the immediate effects were bad enough--my daughters said, "Yechh!" and refused to even set foot in the garage--but when I got to thinking about other possible consequences I had to jump start my old ticker. The mouse could get at the camping gear!!! Now, I could survive, I think, finding a mouse nest-- replete with baby mice--in my sleeping bag. But if it happened to The O'Reilly--well, prolonged screams of that pitch and duration would certainly cause severe hearing impairment and hair follicle damage, and possibly impotence, not to mention total panic within a radius of five miles.

The mouse had to go. I tried to shoo the little devil out, but he (she?) was better at hiding than I was at shooing. So I bought a trap--the standard old mousetrap, the kind that TV mice can easily escape, but that TV cats can't avoid--and set it in the garage.

While holding my bruised fingers under the cold water tap, I made a few comments to the effect that the bleeping trap was made of plastic, not wood like the good ones used to be, and that nobody could set a bleepity bleep plastic trap safely, and that we ought to take some of our bleeping technology to build a mousetrap that wouldn't eat a man's bleep bleep fingers instead of putting some bleep of a bleep on the bleeping moon. I don't think The O'Reilly heard me. She was rushing around closing windows and doors.

A few days later, I found a mouse in the plastic trap. A plastic mouse. I suspect smart-aleck son Tim. The real mouse--if there ever was one--simply disappeared.

We had a mouse in the first house we owned in Spokane, too. Every night that *@#$%^&*! mouse came into our bedroom and tried to gnaw his way through the wall behind a bureau. I think he owned a miniature chain saw, from the amount of noise he made. He interrupted our sleep and other important night-time activities indiscriminately. One night, when he began sawing at a particularly inopportune time, I stormed out of bed and moved the dresser away from the wall, intending mayhem.

I forgot I had no shoes--or anything else--on. The mouse began running hither and thither. The O'Reilly and the mouse both thought I was trying to stomp him, but actually I was trying to keep him from biting my feet. The O'Reilly later told me, when she quit giggling and got her breath, that I looked and danced much like a Maori shaman. I don't know how she got to be an authority on Maoris.

The mouse and I did a couple of sets of Maori medicine dance and a waltz or two, then one or the other of us made a misstep, and my foot came down where the mouse already was. As I held up the poor, squashed mouse by the tail, The O'Reilly interrupted her hysterical laughter long enough to point to me and gasp, "Oh, Great White Hunter!!" Me and Rodney Dangerfield--no respect.

In early 1974, son Steve was showing off on a bicycle and fell on his head. The accident wouldn't have been so bad, probably, if he hadn't had so far to fall. He was six foot three. After a month in Intensive Care, he came out of it and recovered fast, even graduating with his high school class, and by October he was pretty fully recovered, even having the permanent plate in his head.

The grandparents and aunts and uncles, though, weren't convinced that he was all right, so he and I planned a quick trip up to Montana and Idaho to show him off to them. Besides, he and I needed a vacation, and the World's Fair was in Spokane, Washington that year. We had planned to stay in Dad's little house in Charlo, since Dad had been in a nursing home for a year or so, and his house hadn't been entered, much less lived in, for months. By people, that is. There had been mice, Steve and I found out, because the evidence was everywhere. Hunters call it sign. There was sign on the

floor, in the cupboards, in the dishes, on the furniture--
everywhere.

Before I could get supper, I had to clean the stove.
And before I cleaned the stove, I had to clean the sink.
We had to wash the chairs before we could sit down, and
the table before we could set it. Then we had to wash the
dishes before we could put food in them. We got all that
done and swept the floor. We picked up several dustpans
full of sign. When I reminded Steve what the dust that
we were breathing actually was, he insisted that we redo
the chairs, the table, the dishes, the stove--everything.
Next morning, he complained about how hard it was to
sleep with rice in his bed, but when he began plucking
the grains of "rice" off his body and found they were were
of the dark brown and sticky variety--well, I wonder
where he learned that kind of language.

It's been hard to convince Steve that mice are
harmless.

When I was a kid, the granary on the home place
seldom had much grain in it, but it had a tremendous
population of mice. Most of them lived to a ripe old age,
because our barn cats were too lazy and too well fed to do
the mice any damage.

When I was just entering my teens, and the
weather was just too cold or too miserably wet or
otherwise not fit for man or beast (September to May, in
Montana), I used to sit for hours in the granary with my
"air rifle" and play Big Game (Mouse) Hunter. Actually,
the air rifle was neither powered by air nor was it a rifle.
It was really a spring musket which shot BBs with a
velocity somewhere between a fast walk and a slow run.
I'd sit there in this cold and gloomy granary, still as a
mouse, and when a Big Game Animal came out, I'd let
him have it. The air rifle would kill a mouse--provided
the range was no more than eight feet and provided that
the BB hit him right behind the ear. A hit any other
place only made him jump straight up and squeal. He'd
run back to his hole and send his missus out to get the
groceries, complaining about his war wounds and
rheumatism, no doubt.

179

One day toward the middle of March, my friend Murdie came over and we spent a whole morning in the granary. Mouse hunting was the one sport I could beat Murdie in--after all, I'd been practicing all winter--so he got bored after a while, and insisted we do something else. When the rain let up in the afternoon, we went walking out across the fields looking for more exciting adventures. Out in the alfalfa fields, the field mice had made runs under the dead grass during the winter. We called them "granny mice", but I have since learned that they are really voles. Now that the snow was melted off, we could see these tunnels, and we set my dog to chasing mice. Watching her soon got to be boring, too, so we got a shovel and began digging our own.

We skinned out a few of the little critters, and each of us covered all our fingers with mouse-skins. What do you do, now, that's more interesting than that ? One of us, I forget which, said, "I wonder how a mouse steak would taste?" and before either of us came to our senses, we'd gotten to the "I will if you will" stage, so, naturally, we couldn't back out.

We each chose a nice haunch of mouse-meat. We'd forgotten that we didn't have any facilities--or even fuel--to cook with, but why should that stop us? We had some kitchen "strike anywhere" matches. The wind blew the matches out as soon as the flare from the head was gone, so we'd strike each match and hold it up close to the mouse haunch quickly before it blew out. That way we got all the sulfur from the match head on the blackened outside of the "steak", which probably improved the flavor some. When we ran out of matches, we declared the steaks done and ate them.

Ever eat a mouse steak? No? Well, you ain't missed much.

Twenty-five years or so later, just before he retired from the Air Force, I looked Murdie up, and we reminisced about the good times--the frosty outhouses, the coasting on the Coulee Hill, the time the bus tipped over--and some of the bad times, too, but Murdie said he

couldn't remember eating mouse steak! I didn't believe
him. That's something nobody could ever forget!

Pamela's Rabbit

Pamela lives next door to me.
Pamela's eight and her brother's three.
Pamela visits, and when she comes,
She brings me lettuce and sometimes plums.

Pamela still has her Easter bunny.
It's all grown up, but its ears go funny.
Pamela visits her every day
And takes her out of her pen to play.

Pamela's rabbit is snowy white.
That's how we can find her late at night.
Pamela's rabbit likes to roam.
Let her out and she won't stay home.

Pamela's rabbit is easy to catch,
But rabbits will kick and will even scratch
When strangers touch them. So I just wait
And call to Pamela over the gate.

Pamela's rabbit is soft and sleek;
Pamela holds her up to her cheek
And babytalks till the bunny's quiet.
Maybe some day I should try it.

Pamela's mother says that she
May buy one more for company.
But I know this 'bout rabbit habits:
There's no such thing as just two rabbits.

A Part of the Desert

Walker stood on the highest rock of the jumble that passes for a mountain in that part of the Mojave. In every direction he could see more piles of rocks, thrusting up from the desert floor where the Spanish Dagger and Joshua Tree compete with creosote bush and mesquite. Everywhere the desert floor was green. It was the greenest April he'd ever seen in the Monument. The heavy winter rains had lasted until March, and the sleeping plants had responded heroically with five or six times their normal growth. Just below him, a juniper clung to the rocks, gaining strength from God knows where. Its outer twigs were blue with berries, making it look like an over-trimmed Christmas tree.

Walker raised his face to the sun and closed his eyes, enjoying his aloneness. A breeze whispered in the juniper, and overhead a raven croaked once as it passed. The rest was silence. Walker inhaled, long and slowly, the odors he loved: dust and sage, creosote and juniper, even rodent urine were spices on the desert's breath. His sweat-soaked shirt felt almost cold in the dry air, but the sun burned on his face and his exposed arms, and a single drop of perspiration trickled down to salt the corner of his mouth.

He stood awhile absorbing the scene, then slid down the rocks to the juniper and sat on a ledge in its shade. The flies that had buzzed around his face on the climb returned to plague him. They sought water, any water, even sweat. He wiped his face with his shirttail, but still they pestered him. He leaned back against the boulder and ignored them. They were a part of the desert and the desert was his soul-balm.

Below him, just above the valley floor, another raven sailed in circles, flapping occasionally. Others called, and Walker saw a whole flock coasting in the updraft, playing in it, wheeling and turning as if in pure enjoyment.

He pulled at the grass beards embedded in his socks. Every place they touched his ankles there would be an angry red blotch tomorrow. Cleaning them out wouldn't do much good; as soon as he started again, the socks would harvest more. Still, the simple mechanical task stilled his mind, like meditation. Already the anger and frustration that had driven him here were fading from his mind.

He felt a little guilty. He shouldn't have yelled at Marge that way. She wasn't a jealous wife. She had no reason to be, but the crack about his secretary had just been the last straw. He should have told Marge where he was going, no matter what. And he should have told his boss why he had to take off so suddenly when things were so busy. But Christ! How could he? He didn't know why himself. All he knew was that Sunday he'd be forty years old, and that his whole Goddam life was a bust. Oh, sure! He had all his hair; he hadn't gone to flab; he still had his first wife; his kids were straight. He even liked his job and his boss. But something was wrong. He'd expected excitement in his life, and it had never happened. Some of his friends were on their second or third wives, or living on boats with girls half their age. He was forty years old and had never been anywhere or done anything. Why? What the hell was wrong with him?

He knew he should start back. He was a long way from his car and an even longer way from his camp. He had walked and climbed all morning and half the afternoon to get this far. He looked down at the rocky mountainside. He could take the easy slope down--the way he'd come. That trail was longer and far out of the way, but it was safer than climbing down the rocks. It would be dark by the time he reached his car, but that wouldn't bother him. The moon was already up and he'd be able to walk in the moonlight tonight.

On the other hand, he could cut diagonally down the mountain to the trail a mile or so to the west. That trail led directly to his car. But the whole mountain face was a pile of huge rocks, and even downhill was heavy going. It was shorter, though.

Bluejays arguing in the brush below him attracted his attention. Curiosity--not the nature of the trails--made his decision. He started down the mountain toward the birds and the well-marked trail.

The short rest had stiffened his muscles. Instead of skipping down the rockslide as he'd pictured himself, he found he had to climb laboriously down each boulder. Even when his muscles loosened and the sweat broke out again, he felt clumsy. His reluctant legs and spongy knees told him that he was more tired than he'd thought. More cautious now, he often took the long way down a rock face, and sometimes back-trailed rather than trust his failing reflexes. He was almost to the trail, and was crossing the last ridge of boulders, when he stepped on a large loose stone, felt it roll, and tried to recover. The stone surface crumbled under his foot. He teetered a moment, arms flailing, then his boot slipped again, slid between rocks and caught. His momentum threw him backward to the ground.

The fall knocked the wind out of him.

An eternity later, when he could breathe again, he cautiously examined himself for damage. Everything moved, except one leg. The loose boulder had rolled down with him and trapped his foot. When he pulled at it, agony washed over him; sweat broke from his face and legs and shoulders. Something must be broken, though he hadn't felt it when he fell.

He looked toward the imprisoned foot. The leg was in a cleft between rocks, a foot or so above ground, with a two-foot boulder wedged above it, barely touching the boot. but making an effective trap. No way to pull free, no way to move the boulder, at least from this position. He tried to sit up, but the cold-sweat pain came again. He lay back, panting, and let the pain ebb away.

He knew how close he was to the trail. It was only a few yards away, behind a six-foot wall of rocks. Anyone passing on the trail wouldn't be able to see him but they could hear him when he called. If anyone passed. This was what--Thursday? On the weekend, there would be lots of people in the desert looking at its bloom. The trail was well-used. Certainly, no later than Saturday morning he'd be found, he told himself. All he had to do was survive until then. How long? Thirty-six hours?

He tried to close his mind against the thirst. Think of anything else, he told himself, but he thought only of water. Eventually, his thoughts went to the sea, and, imagining himself afloat, he drifted into something nearing sleep.

The sun was setting when he woke. He watched the rocks around him change from blazing white to gold to gray. Even before sundown, the moon pressed a silver heel-print in the sky. The desert night would soon be cold. He struggled with his shirt, and after much painful writhing managed to twist free. His back was bare against the ground, but the shirt made a skimpy blanket.

The desert wakened when the sun went down. Faint rustlings told Walker of the moving residents, but for a while he didn't see them. Then he heard a hurried thumping, and a half-grown rabbit scurried through a gap between rocks. It stopped, looked about, shuddered, moved a few drunken steps, shook its head, pawed at its whiskers. Walker lay still, glad for even a rabbit's company. It was almost within reach of his arm when it crouched, then fell over. Its legs jerked once, twice, then it was still.

A scraping sound came from the cleft in the rock beyond the rabbit. Walker strained to look and saw the rabbit's killer. A spade-shaped head slid out of the shadows, riding a few inches above the sand, so close that Walker could see details of the flicking tongue. A diamondback! A huge one! A chill swept over Walker. He hardly dared to breathe.

The snake ignored him. Tongue flashing, it trailed the rabbit. Slowly, it moved to the body, examined it all over. Like a gloating big-game hunter, Walker thought. The snake seized the head, and writhing gently, pulled the body straight. It surged forward and engulfed the rabbit's nose. Walker watched, breathless. A second spasm came. The snake's mouth moved a tiny fraction of an inch farther around the head. A wait. A spasm. Another wait, another spasm. With each surge a tiny bit less rabbit showed. The act was mesmerizing.

When, finally, the rabbit was a pregnant bulge in the rattler's length, Walker felt that he hadn't breathed in a long time. He must have. The sun was gone and the moon hung in a spangled curtain.

The snake lay sated and moribund where it had fed, so close that Walker dared not move. Each time he dozed and woke he looked; the snake was there. The moon set, and in the starlight the rattler was a lump of earth. Still the sour reptilian odor told Walker the snake hadn't moved.

In time, the Eastern stars began to fade. Walker woke and lay dead-still, watching the sky lighten and the rocks around him turn to gold as the morning swept the desert. When the sun had risen high enough to touch and warm him, it also warmed the snake. The reptile slid away until it lay broadside to the sun. Walker wished he could do the same. Throughout the night he hadn't dared even to shiver. As slowly as he could, watching for movement from the snake, he inched himself toward the light. The sun felt good, but he wondered about his trapped leg. He thought it must not be hurt too badly; it hadn't pained him in the night. He moved his toes and a million needles stung his leg and foot. Straining to keep from moving suddenly, he flexed his foot again and again, steeling himself against the agony of returning circulation. It took a while. He knew the feeling had returned when the grass barbs biting on his ankles began to itch.

The thirst obsession came again in the heat of mid-morning. He tried to lick his lips, but found his tongue too dry to do much good. The sun-baked half of him was sweating, though he tried to shade it with his shirt. God, how he'd love to have some water.

He'd think of something else. He looked over at the snake, now resting in the shade of the rocks. It was

187

colored like the earth, and the diamond pattern of its scales that gave its name was muted so it hardly showed at all. It might have been a stone, a mound of earth, until it moved. The unwinking eye might be watching him--or it might not. The reptile seemed so harmless. Yet Walker had heard that the bite of a diamond-back of this size could kill a man in two hours. He hoped it would go away.

The sun dragged through the sky. Thirst pressed on him, choking him with his own gluey tongue. He cursed his stupidity for getting himself into such a fix. He'd left home angry, and they had no idea where he was. No, that wasn't right. Marge knew he would come to the desert. It had always been his refuge. But she would not know when to expect him back, and he might die before she thought him overdue. No! He would not die! Today was Friday, and tomorrow help would come.

The day crawled on. He studied the rocks to pass the time. The veins of quartz intermingled with the softer layers had always intrigued him. He had often wondered how they'd been formed, but had never spent any time in serious study. The boulders, lying in their crazy puzzles, were a curiosity to be accepted for what they were. They'd trapped him here, sure, but it was his fault, not their doing.

He watched an ant climb up a spear of grass, reach the top, find no place to go, and climb back down. A walking-stick moved slowly in the shade of the rocks toward some destination Walker couldn't see. The snake lay in the shade, moving as the sun moved, always staying in the shadow. Eventually, the day was over.

Sundown brought the evening chill, but with it Walker's thirst slackened a bit. The snake was near again. It had come out from under the rocks to catch the last rays of the sun. Walker moved carefully to cover himself with his shirt against the night.

It's Friday night, he thought. Tomorrow there'll be people. Tomorrow I'll be rescued, surely. He counted stars to go to sleep.

Marge was in his office. She'd been downtown and had stopped in to ask for his opinion. Then Kathy barged in--no knock, no apology. Marge had not met Kathy yet. Walker noticed that his wife's eyes narrowed.

"Kathy," he said, "this is my wife. Marge, this is Kathy Lang. She's my new secretary."

Neither woman said anything--they just looked each other over. Walker felt awkward, and somehow guilty. Then Kathy smiled, showing too many too perfect teeth, excused herself and turned to leave. Walker noticed the pretty little flirt of her pretty little behind before she shut the door. Marge turned back to him, but seemed to have forgotten why she came. The pupils of her eyes were vertical slits, like the snake's.

Walker woke to moonlight in his face. Something was pressing against the underside of his trapped leg. At first, he thought it was a cramp, but it moved from no will of his. Without looking, he knew it was the snake. He'd heard of this--the reptile seeking warmth in the cold night. Before today, he would have been terrified. Tonight he only hoped. He'd gladly give whatever warmth he had to keep the snake from striking.

At last the snake lay still. After a long time, Walker was able to accept its presence, and sleep. He woke and dozed and woke again at intervals all through the night. The snake lay still as death against his thigh.

With the coming of the morning sun, the snake moved away again. Walker tensed and relaxed his muscles to relieve the cramps that came from total stillness through long the night. He felt cheery even though his thirst was choking him. Saturday. Rescue day. He'd made it, snake, thirst and all.

Walker only knew when the snake moved into the shade because he heard it. His eyes were feeling thirst now, too, and were sometimes hard to focus. He lay still as he could, trying not to think of the sticky cob that was his tongue.

The "whap-whap-whap" of rotor blades identified the helicopter. He heard it for a time before he saw it near the hills, flying at a constant height above the ground. They were looking. For what? For him? Here I am, he thought.

He looked at the snake. It was still to close for him to risk much movement. He couldn't even rise up on his elbows, nor move to wave. The chopper flew along the trail, so low that Walker saw the pilot's face. Why did they not see him? Of course! His pants and shirt were tan, the color of the earth. He was a part of the desert, an invisible lump on its face, like the snake.

The helicopter stayed around all afternoon, crisscrossing the desert in its search. Please come back, Walker prayed. I'm here. Please.

Near sundown the rotor sounds faded into silence. Saturday had come and gone and no help had come. Maybe none ever would. Maybe he'd really be a permanent part of the desert--a pile of rags and bones, the color of the sand. His hope was almost gone when he drifted off.

He was in the elevator of his office building. The car was crowded with the evening rush. Kathy stood in front of him, and the pressing crowd pushed him so his hand was held against her body. She turned and smiled at him showing those perfect teeth. The smile grew wider, the she laughed, showing fangs just like the snake's. He felt her press against his arm.

The movement was the snake, lying between his body and his arm. What difference did it make? He was going to die here, from thirst or snake bite, it didn't make much difference. He slept again.

Bernie was in Walker's office, looking sad. One of the nicest things about having Bernie for a boss was that Bernie never scolded, never threatened, never raged. When he was disappointed or should be furious, Bernie looked sad. Walker always felt like he'd kicked a dog when he made Bernie look sad.

"I hear they offered you a job," Bernie said.

"Yes," Walker said. How had Bernie found out?

"Will you take it?"

"I think not. It's not enough."

190

"What is enough?" Bernie asked softly. His eyes were like the dying rabbit's. Walker had been with Bernie for fifteen years. He had to turn away.

The moon was almost down. It wasn't long till dawn and heat and thirst.

Kathy beckoned from her door. Her slender body wriggled, the invitation plain. Walker hesitated. What if Marge found out? He couldn't go through that. Kathy moved to him, pressed against him, smiled and clung to him. Her perfect smile enlarged, her mouth became a cavern that moved toward him, swallowed him. The cavern walls were cold and smelled of reptile.

The snake moved--barely--then lay still.

Walker didn't know when the snake left him or when it moved into the shade. Whenever he was conscious, thirst consumed him. His tongue was a wooden stick that filled his mouth. Congealed saliva sealed his throat and choked his swallow. His eyes burned with their dryness, and blurred almost constantly. He knew he hadn't long.

He was walking in the gravel bed of a mountain stream. Rather he was staggering, and Marge was beside him, helping him as he stumbled on the slippery rocks. He could hear the water, but he couldn't seem to find it. He heard the booming of a waterfall, the tinkle of splashing water that sounded like voices. Then he heard the rushing sound like water from a hose.

The warmth of Marge dissolved into sunlight on his arm and shoulder, and the rush of water was the snake. It lay just under a rock, coiled, tense, warning with its rattle. There were thumping feet and voices on the trail! Walker tried to call, but no sound came past his swollen tongue. He worked his mouth desperately to free his voice. So near, and now they'd pass him by.

The footsteps stopped.

"Quiet!" It was a man's voice. The other voices--children's--ceased. The rattler's buzz was the only sound.

"Rattlesnake," the man said, "Stay here." The sound of cautious movement came to Walker. The snake eased farther under the rocks, but kept its rattle going as it slid away. A head and shoulders loomed among the rocks, blurred by Walker's tearless eyes.

"Good God! He's killed this guy! You kids stay there." The man stopped and listened for the snake's position before he dropped down beside Walker

Walker tried to speak, to move. A whisper came, "Wah-er."

"He's alive! Jeff, the canteen." The man scrambled back over the rocks toward the trail. "Bill, run for camp and tell anybody you see we've found the guy the Ranger's looking for. Tell 'em he's snakebit. Move!" Running steps faded on the trail. The man came back, lifted Walker's head, dripped water into his mouth. The musty canteen water was the best that Walker ever tasted. It took a while to swallow past his swollen tongue and sticky throat.

"Enough, now," the man said. "I'll give you more soon's I get the snake."

Walker caught feebly at the man's leg. "No," he managed. "Don't."

The man bent over him. What's that?"

Walker strained to make words. "Not bit. Thirsty. Leg. There." Each word was a gasp. He waved weakly at his trapped foot. "Okay now. Just water."

Far back under the rocks, safe, its rattle still, the snake looked like another mound of sand.

Politically Incorrect

("PORTLAND-- The Oregonian...will stop publishing sport teams names that may be offensive.... References to the Braves, Indians, Redskins, Redmen, will be dropped..."
from the Spokane, Washington *Spokesman Review*, February 15, 1992)

Today it seems Political
Correctness is in style.
We cannot use some of the words
We've used for quite a while.

Minorities speak to their own
In deprecating terms.
But if we others use them, then
They'll treat us just like worms.

Native Americans now say
That the Atlanta **Braves**
Are named in such a way that they
Dishonor old time graves.

And what will happen now if they
Require a change of name?
To watch Atlanta **Bolds** at bat
I fear won't be the same.

The **Red**skins that in D.C. play
Are ever so much worse.
There's talk of boycott of their games
And then an ancient curse.

The **Red**skins? How about we call
Their team the **Sunburned Hoods**?
The Kansas City **Chiefs** will be
The K.C. **Not So Goods**.

And Georgia Tech must change the name
From **Yellow**jackets, too.
Politically correct will say
That **Beige Coats** has to do.

The **Rams** of L.A. must offend
The women's movement deep.
We'll have to call them what they are:
The California **Sheep**.

America's team are the boys
That down in Dallas live.
The thrill the **Cowboys** used to raise
Will **Bovine Persons** give?

If California South has **Kings**
The North must have a sequel.
In San Francisco we will field
The **Queens** to make it equal.

This stuff is going much to far.
I fear we'll see the day
That baseball umpires have to let
A **Personager** play.

By golly, I know what I'll do.
I'll raise a fuss and say:
The failing **White Sox** out of Chi
Must change their hose to **Gray**.

Inhibitions

I'm not usually intimidated by inanimate objects. People, yes. A brace of burly, belligerent bikers will raise my voice an octave or so, and make me step carefully, but not a "head". Not usually.

The O'Reilly and I were touristing in Seattle a few years ago, doing such things as watching the salmon as they climbed the fish-ladders at the Lake Union locks. I was fascinated by the way those little guys use their fins on those slippery ladder rungs. We'd also made a quick tour through the University District. Somebody must have moved everything around, because I couldn't find any of the places where I remembered them from forty-odd years before.

When it got to be lunch time, we started looking for a sit-down restaurant, since fast food's against my ulcer's principles. We finally found ourselves crossing Lake Union on the University Bridge, and then on Eastlake Avenue on the South side. Right there, below the freeway (200 feet below the freeway) was a small restaurant that looked like our style--quiet and plain. So we parked and went inside, and--oh boy--how our style changed.

The place was done in black and chrome. The walls were twenty feet high and were hung with huge mirrors and expensive paintings and trophy fish. Bottle after bottle of fine booze sat on the shelves in front of the mirrors. The waiters wore tuxedos--at noon on a Tuesday, yet. Intimidated? Not me. My plastic's as good as anybody's.

The maitre d' rushed right over and offered us a table where we could look out at Lake Union and watch the boats go by. We had an unspoken agreement--I didn't make fun of his tuxedo, and he didn't make fun of my fishy blue jeans.

After we ordered, I went to "wash my hands". That's when I became intimidated.

Back in my Navy days I went to a fancy theater in San Francisco. Movies were free to servicemen, and I haven't been to such a nice theater since. There in their rest room was a nice, friendly gentleman wearing a tuxedo. He handed me a towel, and while I was drying my hands he started to brush off my shoes. I thought maybe I'd dribbled on my feet, and when he took a whisk-broom and brushed off shoulders, I thought, "Gosh, I sure must have got dirty in here." When I finished with the towel, he held out his hand, and gee, he seemed like a fine fellow, so I shook it.

Since then, I've been in "men's rooms" from east to west, north to south, and all in between. Some had cathedral ceilings; some had no ceilings at all. Some had mosaic tile floors; some had sagging wood floors that seemed like they were about to collapse. Some had fine paintings on the walls; some had fifty years of graffiti on the walls.

This Seattle john, though, was the like of which I'd never seen. It had chrome and black and mirrors, sure, but I'd seen those before. But--

Most modern men's rooms have individual urinals; the trough urinal is passe. This place had a trough, but what a trough!! It was shiny, dark blue enamel, maybe ten inches deep. It was piled with mounds of tiny ice cubes, shaped into crystalline mountains, and overhead, blue spotlights were focussed on the ice. It gave the effect of looking down on the Olympic Peninsula in the moonlight.

Above the trough hung a huge bulletin board, and pinned to the board were the important pages of the Seattle Post-Intelligencer: the front page, the sports page and the comics pages. I had visions of a Monday morning there after the Seahawks or the Mariners had had a particularly impressive win, (or ANY win, for that matter) with all the Monday morning quarterbacks JOCKeying for position to read the sports page. Or, more probably, the FRONT page of the P-I., if the Mariners or Seahawks managed to win. Maybe in Seattle they're fast readers, or maybe they have a lot of kidney problems there, but I couldn't imagine standing there even long enough to read the comics.

As a matter of fact, I couldn't imagine standing there at all. Ruin those pretty blue mountains ? I just couldn't do it. I went into a stall and peed in the commode.

Beach Mama
(A Rap Poem)

I be chillin'[1] at the beach with a ice cold beer
A'hawkin'[2] at the hotties[3] runnin there and here
When a fly-girl[4] wiggles by that's real down[5] def[6]
An I wonder should I bust-a-move[7] an not get left
And I be maybe hooked up[8] with a mama that's fresh.
Then a hard[9] dude DaddyMac[10] shows up in the flesh.
He be out from the hood[11] with his posse[12] at his charge.
He be frontin'[13] for the B-girl[14] like he livin' large[15].
He ain't got lotsa cake;[16] I know it for a fact.
Now the fly-girl's a'clocking[17] an I see she's feelin'
    wacked[18].
I figure that he illin'[19] cause he's dissin[20] her for sure.
I ain't down[21] with his act but I know there's a cure.

---

[1] relaxing
[2] staring at a member of the opposite sex
[3] attractive females
[4] attractive girl
[5] approved
[6] outstanding
[7] take some action
[8] introduced
[9] tough
[10] playboy type
[11] inner city
[12] group of friends
[13] showing off
[14] rap fan
[15] financially successful
[16] like he has lots of money
[17] noticeably upset
[18] feeling bad
[19] being absurd
[20] disrespectful, harassing
[21] I don't approve

Well, he start to sweatin[22] her so I pull out my piece[23]
An tell him to chill[24] cause this gotta cease
An I tell him step off[25] and step off NOW
Or this piece might go off an hurt him somehow.
Then the lady turn an give me a stupid-fresh[26] smile
An now she's be a home-girl[27]. Least for a while.

---

[22] giving her a hard time
[23] handgun
[24] relax, calm down
[25] get out of my face
[26] really great-great
[27] friend

Past Actions Haunt You ?
Dissatisfied With Your Performance ?

AT LAST !

PICA PROCESSOR POWER COMES TO YOUR AID

No Longer need you expend your valuable energy and time lamenting your regrettable deeds. Now, you can leave all that to

THE 2-B REGRETTOR

The Waglance 2-B Regrettor regrets your financial, business, social, moral and personal misdeeds or decisions for you. The Regrettor regrets with the intensity and level required by your own perception of the consequences of your regrettable act. YOU set the parameters and the 2-B does the rest.

The 2-B Regrettor can be held in and programmed by one hand. Controls are capacitive touch buttons, except for the LEVEL control, which is a screw operated variable capacitor controlled by a rotating knob. This construction and a power source guaranteed for the life of the unit ensure exceptional reliability. The 2-B Regrettor is a triumph of pica-processor technology at an affordable price.

See your local distributor, now!

WAGLANCE
The SPIAN Group
1573 Stratford Avenue
Elizabeth RI

MODEL 2-B REGRETTOR CONTROLS AND OPERATION

The 2-B Regrettor is easily programmed for proper regretting. Mode and submode controls set the regret type and cause. Magnitude and level controls then modify the intensity and total regret

BUNGLE MODE Select

BUNGLE MODE provides for the selection of the facet of your life most affected by the regrettable action. MODE selections are mutually exclusive, although allowances are made in each MODE for regrets which will probably associate between MODES. The basic Model 2-B contains pica-processors for six modes:

    BUSINESS
    FINANCIAL
    MORAL
    LEGAL
    SOCIAL
    PERSONAL

Associative regret probabilities are preset at the factory, but a fine-tuning algorithm--based on the frequency of use of each MODE--modifies the association parameters. Thus, for instance if the MORAL MODE is never used, the MORAL regret associated with each of the other modes will diminish gradually, eventually being eliminated altogether.

The MODE processors and their associated touch buttons are field replaceable units. Other processors are under development, notably a SEXUAL MODE which is expected to be in great demand by those of middle age who missed the sexual revolution.

BOTCH CLASS Submode Select

BOTCH CLASSES loosely reflect the major causes for regrettable acts and decisions. The 2-B provides selection of:

CONCUPISCENCE
OMISSION
TWISTED TONGUE
FREUDIAN SLIP
POOR TIMING
CONCLUSION JUMP
FOOT-IN-MOUTH
LIE
DAMN LIE
IGNORANCE
INCOMPETENCE
SHEER, UNADULTERATED STUPIDITY

Where BOTCH CLASSES are obviously mutually inclusive or exclusive, the 2-B allows selection of only one CLASS. Priority is given to those classes lower on the list. Thus, if CONCLUSION JUMP and IGNORANCE are both selected, IGNORANCE will be used by the Regrettor. If, however, POOR TIMING and DAMN LIE are both selected, both will be used, since the regrettability of a damn lie generally depends on the timing.

FAULT MAGNITUDE Control

This control allows the user to select his own estimate of the seriousness of the results of the regrettable act. Mutually exclusive FAULT MAGNITUDES, in order of increasing severity, are:

FAUX PAS
EMBARRASSMENT
HUMILIATION
CATASTROPHE
TOTAL RUIN
DAMNATION

The selections are only indicative. The connotations of TOTAL RUIN are quite different for MORAL and BUSINESS regrets.

AMELIORATION LEVEL Control

The amount one wishes to regret a particular act is a personal choice. The regret expended is a function of the MAGNITUDE integrated over time, the time being a relative function proportional the the AMELIORATION LEVEL setting. This control is continuously adjustable from minimum to maximum regret, with approximate LEVELS indicated at:

SALVE CONSCIENCE
EXCUSE SELF
FORGET IT
ABSOLUTION
TOTAL VINDICATION

WAGLANCE believes that to "regret forever" an act or decision is self-destructive. The TOTAL VIDICATION (maximum) setting is therefore designed to expunge even an infinitely regrettable act efficaciously.

Truth

Once I was younger and was wise,
And absolutely knew
Some things in life were surely false,
And some were surely true.

Truth always came in white or black,
And never in between.
But then in time my truths began
To fade and now are seen

To be deceptive. Some I've found
Are false as they can be.
And things that I once knew were false
Are now the truth, I see.

Perhaps about my truths I'll find
That now I am mistaken.
I've been wrong once. I've been wrong twice.
New thoughts new truths awaken.

So now, my child, if I propound
The Truth to you today
Remember: always question
The truth in I what say.

BUILDING CHARACTER

TALES FROM MONTANA

(and Other Damn Lies)

ORDER FROM

Polecat Press
612 West Haycraft
Coeur d' Alene, Idaho
83814

BUILDING CHARACTER

First Book (Price $7.95, plus $2.05
Shipping, Handling, and sales tax)　　　$10.00

_____ Additional Books @ 7.95 ea. (Inc-
ludes prepaid shipping, handling, taxes)　_____

TOTAL　　　　　　　　　　　　　$_____

Check or Money Order only, please.